The King of
Devil's Canyon

Clint Ellsworth

DEDICATION

To every kid that wants to find joy in the
outdoors,
this book is for you.

And
because I like you so much…
I made you hunting
videos, stories, and products at
TrueHunter.com

CONTENTS

INVITATION

Hunting is one of the most exciting things in the world. Some of the most thrilling moments of my life came while hunting as a kid with a parent or mentor. As an adult, my most sensational moments hunting have been with my kids!

I created the True Hunter Lucky Coin to inspire both young and old. This coin is an important 'character' of all my True Hunter books. If the story of James and Jack touches your heart, I invite you to get a free silver-plated Lucky Coin with any additional purchase at **TrueHunter.com**.

Just add a Lucky Coin to your cart and use the code FREECOIN at checkout to receive my gift to you!

CHAPTER 1

FIRST HUNT

I will never forget the day I became a hunter. I can still feel the way the crisp September air felt on my face early that morning almost 4 years ago. I remember how my lungs burned while trying to keep up with my dad. We were bull elk hunting together in a place called Devil's Canyon. It was the first time that I was old enough to go hunting with my dad. I'd waited my whole life to go on my first hunt, and I was so excited that it was with him.

My dad is my hero, and there is no one who I'd rather spend time with. But after hours of hiking in the cold dark forest, I could see why he made me wait so long to come with him. Hunting was hard! The forest floor was slippery with the morning dew. There was no flat ground. It was either uphill or downhill, and I kept slipping. My knees were wet from tripping and falling so many times, but I was determined to not let my dad see me struggle. I laughed in my head that Dad chose to take me to a place called "Devil's Canyon" on my first hunt. At first, I wondered why they called it that, but then it became obvious. The rocks were sharp, and there were steep cliffs everywhere. If I wasn't so brave, I would have even called it terrifying....

I had barely turned 8 years old. I wanted to prove to Dad that he didn't make a mistake by taking me with him. I'd been begging him to take me hunting for years. He always told me that when I was old enough, I would get to go with him, but he never said what age "old enough" was. Last year I had gotten so upset when he told me I couldn't go on his deer hunt. I cried myself to sleep that night.

Dad surprised me last week when he handed me a small box with camouflage wrapping paper. I tore open the wrapping paper as fast as I could. My eyes lit up when I saw a new pair of camouflage pants. He told me that I would need them to be able to go with him on his muzzleloader bull elk hunt. I hopped up off the couch, and jumped on him. He totally fell over and landed on his big comfy chair. I wrapped my arms around his neck, and gave him the biggest hug.

The morning of the hunt, Mom woke me up super early to get dressed before Dad and I made our drive to Devil's Canyon. It was pitch-black outside. I had never gotten dressed when it was still dark outside before. I put on the camouflage pants that Dad had given me. They fit perfectly. Then I put on a long sleeve camo shirt, but my favorite part of the morning was when Dad smeared black, brown and green camouflage paints on my face.

When he was done, he joked with me and said, "James? Where did you go? I don't see you anymore! James! James! Where are you?"

I laughed and said, "I'm right in front of you Dad."

He laughed even harder and smiled really big. "With all that camouflage on I couldn't see you anymore!"

He was such a fun dad. He was always joking around with me. But now we were on the hunt, and he was being more serious than normal. He kept on looking back at me to make sure I was still behind him. He said we had to move fast to get to a special spot before the sun came up.

It was so hard to move fast and be quiet at the same time. There were dead trees that had fallen down all over the place. Dad said that they were called "Deadfall". It felt like there were thousands of these giant trees laying on the ground. We had to climb over them. It was a lot easier for my dad to get over the dead trees. His legs were a lot longer than mine were. He could just step over them. I basically had to climb over each one!

When we finally got to the spot Dad had in mind, I was completely out of breath. I looked around to see what was so special about this place. To me it looked like the rest of the forest that we had hiked through.

I whispered to Dad, "So why this spot?"

He smiled and pointed behind us. We were sitting on a hill, and about 30 yards above us there was a well used elk trail.

He said, "Do you see that opening along that worn out trail? The elk love to walk along that trail early in the morning while they make their way to a nearby water hole. That opening in the trees should give us a clear shot, if they decide to come down the trail this morning. Right here is a great place to sit and listen. Lean up against this big pine tree, and let me know if you hear anything."

I heard the leaves on the aspen trees rustling. The leaves were turning the most amazing bright colors. I almost felt like I was in a painting.

I heard chipmunks. I looked around and found a chipmunk standing on a log going about his daily business as if we weren't even there.

"Chipmunks look like mice wearing tuxedos," I whispered.

Dad grinned, but put his finger to his lips. "Shhh, now isn't the time to talk."

I heard squirrels that sounded as big as elephants! For reals. They chased each other in the leaves, and they made so much noise! I couldn't believe how loud they were. Didn't they know that Dad said to be quiet... but I did not hear anything that sounded like an elk.

I looked at the big gun my dad was carrying. Dad told me that it was called a muzzleloader, because you loaded it through the barrel. I thought that was silly. It should be called a "barrel loader" if you loaded it through the barrel.

This type of gun looked a lot more old fashioned than the other guns Dad had. This one looked like it was from 100 years ago. It even had a cool hammer mechanism on it that you pull back when you are ready to shoot. The hammer crashes down when you pull the trigger. It creates a spark. That spark creates an explosion inside the gun and pushes out a lead ball. It was pretty complicated if you asked me. My .22 I got for my birthday would have been a lot easier to use.

I didn't hear anything else, but I did feel the wind coming down off the mountain. I guess that's why we set up below the trail instead of above it. Dad was always talking about how an elk can smell a human from hundreds of yards away. You never want to sit in a place where the wind takes your scent to the elk. I sniffed my armpits. Yep. They stunk. Glad we were sitting down wind from the trail.

I started to get bored. We walked so fast and so hard to get to this spot, and now all we were doing was sitting. Dad told me I needed to be as motionless as possible. I decided that sitting still was not my favorite part about hunting. While we were sitting Dad let me hold his grunt tube. It's this plastic tube that is supposed to help you sound more like an elk when you call into it.

His grunt tube looked like an old-fashioned trumpet covered in camouflage. Bull elk communicate with each other by bugling. Bugling is the most amazing sound. It starts with a deep growl, and then gets super high pitched really fast. Hunters try to sound like they are a bull elk to trick the real life bulls into coming close enough to shoot. At home Dad was always practicing his bugle. Mom hated it. Our neighbors probably hated it too. It was really, really loud.

I thought it was awesome! He had this special plastic thing that he put into his mouth called a diaphragm. Almost like magic, he could create cool noises that sounded like a bull elk. But, whenever I bugled, I would just use my natural voice. I didn't need the plastic thingy. My mouth was too small for it, and it made me gag when I tried using one! I just used my voice, and made the sounds my dad made. I had never actually heard a bull elk bugle in real life, but Dad told me I sounded just like an elk.

At that moment, a great idea came into my mind! I whispered to Dad, "Can I do a bugle right now?"

My dad's eyes got really big like he wasn't sure how to answer. I'd seen that look so many times before on his face. Especially whenever mom asked him to do something that he really didn't want to do. Kind of like the time she asked him to take out the trash during an intense football game on TV.

Luckily, he nodded his head and whispered, "Go for it big guy. Let those bull elk know there's a challenger in the woods this morning."

I licked my lips, and took a big deep breath. I put the grunt tube up to my mouth, and started to make a low growl sound. Then I changed the sound to a really high-pitched shriek, almost like a yell. I finished my bugle with a hiccup-like sound that bull elk sometimes make at the end of their bugles. Dad looked at me as proud as a dad could look at his son. I beamed with pride. Then I heard a branch snap behind me, and my heart jumped....

CHAPTER 2

BULL LEAPING

I whipped my head backwards to look around the big pine tree that we were hiding behind. A big cow elk entered the clearing exactly where Dad told me it would.

I turned to look at Dad and whispered intently, "Dad, Dad, Dad, there's an elk!"

He smiled as if I was joking with him. He didn't believe me! He was watching a couple of squirrels chase each other down below us.

I grabbed his arm, and pulled him towards me. Suddenly, he realized I was being serious. He stealthily looked around the tree, and saw not one but two cow elk walking along the path! Dad put up two fingers to let me know what he saw. He grabbed his muzzleloader, and got into a kneeling position. He pulled the muzzleloader up to his shoulder. He used the tree trunk to help keep the gun still. He kneeled right next to me.

Dad whispered to me, "A lot of times a bull will push cow elk in front of him to keep them going where he wants them to go."

I watched, I hoped, I wished that a bull would step out next. At that moment a terrifying shriek came from behind the cows. It was a bugle! It was an angry bugle. It was the first real elk bugle I had ever heard. It was absolutely incredible! My dad's eyes got huge. My eyes got huge. He pulled the hammer back on the muzzleloader. He got ready to shoot. My heart was thumping so hard in my chest that I worried the elk could hear it!

Then it happened. The angry bull stepped into the opening. His antlers seemed to reach to the top of the trees.

Dad tried to aim, but for some reason he was shaking like a leaf on a windy day. The barrel was shaking too. He pulled the trigger. The muzzleloader violently kicked back into his shoulder. The sound of the black powder exploding felt like a punch to my ears. I was shaken from the blast. In half a daze I looked up at the bull. His back legs didn't seem to be working anymore. Dad had hit him in the spine! The wounded bull elk lost his balance, and began to roll down the hill straight towards us.

At that moment I had visions of greatness and glory. I was going to jump over the bull as it rolled directly into my path. I would be a legend! How many people have ever jumped over a rolling elk? I was going to do it. I had it timed. I went to leap up and out of nowhere....

My dad grabbed me, and pulled me out of the way just as the bull rolled where I had been ready to jump. He rolled to a stop a few yards below us, where he hit a big pine tree trunk. The giant tree shook from the weight of the bull slamming into it. Pine cones fell from the tree like rain.

Dad frantically tried to reload the muzzleloader. His hands were shaking, and he had a hard time putting the black powder down the barrel. He quickly took the ramming rod, and pounded the lead ball down to the powder. He threw the rod to the side. He pulled back the hammer again and aimed. He shot, and this time he hit the bull right behind the shoulder. Bubbles started to ooze out of the newly formed hole in the side of the bull. He hit him directly in the lungs. The bull lifted his head one last time. His antlers raised high then crashed down to the earth.

Adrenaline rushed through my body. I had witnessed the most epic elk hunting moment in the history of the world. I was so pumped!

Dad gave me a giant hug and exclaimed, "James! You bugled in this amazing bull! I bet no 8-year-old has ever done what you've just done! You are a natural born hunter!"

I smiled ear-to-ear as he spoke those words. I felt his words deep down in my heart. "I am a natural born hunter!"

CHAPTER 3

LUCKY COIN

"That's quite the story, James!" replied Jack, my baseball coach. "I'm impressed! But did you really try to jump over a rolling bull elk?" Jack questioned with a chuckle.

I exclaimed, "I absolutely did, and I totally would have made it if Dad didn't completely ruin the moment! I may have only been 8 years old, but I could jump like a rabbit! I would have cleared that bull no problem. Maybe I would have even done a flip over the bull just to make it a little more interesting...."

My dad looked over at Jack, and rolled his eyes. Dad had brought me over to Jack's house. Jack was his best friend, and an avid hunter.

"Oh James, you have always been pretty confident, huh? Well, I for one, am glad your dad pulled you out of the way, cuz I'm pretty sure that bull would have broken every bone in your body! That bull would have smashed you into a pancake!"

Dad chimed in, "I seriously couldn't believe what I was seeing. This 8-year-old kid of mine was honestly ready to jump. There was no fear in his eyes. It took me a second to realize that he was actually going to try it! I was super lucky that I was close enough to grab him without us both being flattened by that bull."

We laughed together, and then there was a moment when none of us spoke. I looked around Jack's home. It was full of the coolest animal mounts. He had an enormous whitetail buck that had multiple drop tines, a bull elk, a red stag that he shot in New Zealand, and a giant shoulder mount of a moose that he got in Alaska. There was even a full-sized grizzly mount that stood at least 10 feet tall. I'd never seen anything like it. The grizzly had a wicked scar that ran from the bottom of his eye all the way to where his right ear should have been. The grizzly's right ear wasn't even there! It was terrifying.

"So, your dad tells me that you are putting in for the big hunting lottery this year. He said that you're putting in for an archery bull elk hunt. During the rut. In Devil's Canyon. Don't you know Devil's Canyon is the most sought after area to hunt in the state?" Jack said, raising his bushy eyebrows.

"So, what are you trying to say?" I replied.

"You do realize that it is almost impossible to get your name drawn for such a prize hunt, right? I mean I have been putting in for that exact hunt my whole life, and my name has never been drawn. It's actually my dream hunt," stated Jack.

I responded confidently, "Coach, don't you know me by now? I'm always going for the biggest score. Dad and I call it 'Go big or go home'."

"James, you're right," he said, nodding with a smirk on his face.

"You always do go for the biggest score, and I love that about you. No fear whatsoever!"

He paused for a second as if he had a new thought come into his head.

"But… it always helps to have a little luck on your side."

As Jack said that he reached into his pocket slowly, and pulled out a big silver coin. He rolled it over in his big, sunbaked hands. He looked at it for a lingering moment, and then he flipped it over to me. I watched the coin sail high in the air. I reached out with my right hand. I caught it in my palm, and I squoze tightly to make sure it didn't fall to the ground.

"What's this, Jack?" I asked, looking curiously at the coin.

"Well… I want you to have it. The coin is yours now. I've had it since I was 8 years old. My dad gave it to me. It's always brought me luck and helped me see life a little more clearly."

He looked at me with a more serious face when he said, "more clearly".

"I think it will do the same for you. I don't have a kid to hand it down to...." He said that last part with a little tremor in his voice. I could see the pain in his eyes.

He coughed to clear his throat and said, "Maybe it will even help you get drawn for your dream archery bull tag that you put in for."

Wow! What an awesome looking silver coin. I looked it over carefully. On one side, at the bottom of the coin, it said "True Hunter". Above the words it had a giant whitetail buck jumping out of a compass. It looked so cool. I had never seen a coin like this before. It was silver and shiny, and it was surprisingly big! Much bigger than a quarter. But what stood out most to me was the phrase "True Hunter".

Jack was definitely a true hunter in my mind. I could only hope to become a true hunter like him some day. I rolled the coin over in my hand. On the back side, at the top, following the curvature of the coin, were the words "Your Legacy". Under the words there was an older hunter and a younger hunter walking together with their guns. The older hunter had his hand on the young hunter's shoulder. There was a strong sense of a hunter's bond minted into the back of that coin. You could tell that the young hunter and the old hunter felt a special closeness.

I thought about the way I felt when I was in the woods with my dad on our epic elk hunt together. I felt closer to him. Almost like the rest of the world disappeared, and it was just us. I think hunting together with someone else does that to you. It brings you closer to that person.

I smiled really big, and told Jack how much I appreciated the coin. I gave him a super grown up handshake. The kind where you grab someone's hand with your whole hand, and squeeze with a firm grip. I looked Jack in the eyes. I promised him that I'd always have the coin in my pocket, no matter what I was doing.

CHAPTER 4

DREAM LOTTERY

The months passed slowly, but the day of the hunting lottery finally arrived. Dad and I were playing catch outside. We loved to play catch together in our front yard under the shade of our big pine tree.

"Dad, why do they have to have a hunting lottery anyway? Why can't we just hunt wherever and whatever we want to?" I asked.

Dad laughed and said, "That sounds like a better way, doesn't it? The problem is there are a lot of people who want to hunt in these special areas. If everyone hunted whenever and whatever they wanted, the animals would all disappear pretty fast. Each area can only withstand a certain number of hunters each year to maintain healthy numbers of deer and elk. So, the only fair thing to do is draw names for each available spot. Lots of hunters don't get picked, but it makes it really exciting and special when your name does get drawn for the hunt you want."

"Oh man! Please, please, please let me get drawn for my bull elk tag," I shouted at the top of my lungs. Dad laughed pretty hard with me.

I put in for a couple other hunts, but this archery, bull elk hunt, in the rut was the one my heart desired. I really wanted to hunt during the rut, because that is the only time of the year when the bull elk bugle a lot. The rest of the year they are mostly quiet. In my mind, that would not be nearly as exciting.

The state always releases the lottery results towards the end of the day. Once the results are out, about a million people all go on the website at the exact same time to find out if they got drawn or not. It's crazy!

For my family it's bigger than the Super Bowl. We have a party and invite a bunch of friends that can't wait to see if they got drawn. Mom makes her famous guacamole dip. Some guests bring chips, and others bring yummy cheeses. Dad even gets into some cooking action and bakes a cake. Every year he decorates it with something hilarious. Last year he put a skunk figurine on his cake with the words "Not Getting Drawn Stinks" written above the skunk. It was so funny. I couldn't wait to see what he does this year!

After we chat and talk about hunting, we all take turns putting our information into the computer to see the results. If someone does get drawn it's pretty exciting. Everyone yells and makes a huge deal out of it. If you don't get drawn then the crowd is more like a support group. Lots of shoulders to cry on. For real. I have seen adults cry when they don't get drawn! It's the craziest thing.

I was feeling super confident. I had been picturing myself getting drawn for months now. I would imagine the drawing as if it were really happening.

First, I'd take a deep breath, puff out my chest, and strut over to the computer. I pictured everyone looking at me and chanting my name. "James, James, James". Then, I would pull my lucky True Hunter coin out of my pocket, and flip it into the air. It would fly over my head, and then I'd catch it behind my back like a total stud. Then I would kiss the coin, and put on my game face. I'd type my information into the computer, click submit, and see the results. I could see big, bold words going across the computer screen in my mind "**James has been picked to hunt... Devil's Canyon, Bull Elk, Archery, Rut Hunt**." Finally, I pictured myself turning to the waiting crowd, and announcing that I'd been drawn for my #1 dream hunt. Our guests would put me on their shoulders, and I would crowd surf.

It would basically be the most fantastic moment ever. I loved playing this over and over in my head. It always put the biggest grin on my face.

CHAPTER 5

OLD MAN STRENGTH

I had been dreaming about this day for months, but now it was for real. Mom called out to Dad and me while we were still out playing catch. "Hey, you two! Can you get in here and help clean up before everyone gets here?"

Both of us put our heads down and said in unison, "Coming, Mom."

After cleaning up I went outside to wait for people to show up. It was a dreary evening. It was raining and there was some rumbling thunder in the distance. I looked up into the sky and tiny rain droplets hit my face. The sky had turned dark and ominous. I decided to go inside to stay dry.

Not too much later the doorbell started ringing. My parents welcomed each person at the door. Our friends and family shook off their umbrellas on the doorstep and came in. The house started to get louder and louder. The energy they brought into our home was electric. Hope was in the air.

Jack showed up last. He calmly came into the house. He took off his soaking wet jacket, and hung it in the foyer. After he greeted my parents, he made his way over to me.

"James! How's it going buddy? I'm guessing you're pretty excited right about now?"

"Heck yes, I am!" I exclaimed.

I reached down into my pocket, and pulled out the True Hunter coin that he had given me. When I showed it to him, he gave me a warm smile.

"I reckon if you've got your lucky coin then there's nothing to worry about. It really makes me happy to know you have it with you."

"Are you kidding me? It never leaves my side. I even sleep with it in my pajamas!" I said enthusiastically.

Now that Jack had finally shown up my dad decided it was time to reveal his cake creation. He stood up, and calmed the excited crowd. He had put the cake up on the counter with tin foil covering it. No one was allowed to see it until the big reveal. When the crowd had finally hushed, he picked up the cake, and tilted it towards everyone in the room. Mom helped by grabbing the tin foil. She removed it slowly for us all to see….

I burst out laughing!

"Dad, what is that?!" I hollered.

His face turned a little red, and I could tell he felt a bit embarrassed. Then with a booming, half-laughing voice he said, "I tried to draw a big bull elk with cake frosting, but I think it looks a little bit more like a donkey with a tree growing out of its head."

The whole room erupted with laughter. Mom put her head on Dad's shoulder. She started laughing and said, "Honey, I think this is your best cake yet." But she couldn't help but give him a "That was pretty pitiful" look. Dad took it like a champ, and laughed with the rest of the room. Everyone loves my dad. He is so magnetic. You can't help but love the guy.

After a little bit of small talk, everyone started talking about the lottery. The anticipation was killing me, and I wasn't the only one. I saw grown men and women all nervously anticipating the event. As I looked around the room, I noticed how each person showed their nervousness differently.

I saw George, my next-door neighbor, biting his fingernails. I saw Willy, my dentist, nervously tapping his right foot on the tile. I looked over at Jordan, my oldest cousin, his left eye was twitching.

But the funniest sign of nerves came from my favorite aunt, Betty. She kept making frequent trips to the bathroom! She reminded me of my dog when he got too excited. She kept saying, "These drinks are going right through me!" That made me laugh hard.

Dad saw that I noticed her frequent bathroom trips, and he whispered in my ear, "She's always had a nervous bladder!" I laughed out loud. Oh, man I was having the time of my life waiting for the lottery to begin.

Then someone got up and exclaimed, "10 minutes until the lottery results will be live!"

The conversation quickly turned to what order we should check the results. One idea was to draw names out of a hat one by one. Another idea was to do it alphabetically. Then someone came up with the absolutely terrible, awful, horrible, super-lame idea to start from the oldest to the youngest. I happened to be the youngest. Not cool. Not cool at all.

I made my feelings known with fervor. I even jumped up on a chair, and declared to the room that it should be youngest to oldest. I thought I had made a pretty good case for it when up stood the man we all called Papa Bruno. He was like a 100 years old. He had a white beard that went down to his belt. His eyebrows were completely white, and so bushy that they almost covered his dark brown eyes. His ears had gotten really droopy, and they had thick hair growing out of them! The only place he didn't have hair was on the top of his head. He always wore a cowboy hat to keep his bald head covered.

Papa Bruno rolled over on his wheel chair until he was right in front of me. He put his wrinkled, spotted finger in my face and said, "Young man, I'll arm wrestle you for it. If you win, we will go from youngest to oldest. If I win, we will go from oldest to youngest."

The whole room burst into a frenzy. Everything was happening so fast! People started betting on who they thought would win. I couldn't believe it, but my own mom bet against me!

Dad set up a chair for me on one side of the table, and Papa Bruno wheeled his wheelchair to the other side. We clinched hands. We locked eyes. His dark eyes were full of fire.

I felt Bruno squeeze my hand. My hand bones cracked out loud. At that moment, I knew I was doomed. I had made a critical mistake. I had forgotten about "Old Man Strength"!

"Old Man Strength" is the unexplained phenomenon where old gray men suddenly have the strength of a superhero when competing against younger, stronger-looking boys. It's weird, but it's real. And Papa Bruno was as old as a dinosaur, so he was going to be super strong.

I looked over, and saw Jack looking at me. His kind, light blue eyes were wincing as if he knew I was going to get destroyed. So, before my dad could say "GO" to start the arm wrestle contest, I jerked my hand away from Papa Bruno's death grip. I stood up and declared to the room, "I think we should go from oldest to youngest. It's the most honorable thing to do!"

Papa Bruno stood up and said, "Wise choice young man," as he flexed his 100-year-old bicep at me. The whole room laughed loudly.

The truth was I was scared to death of losing. I didn't want to lose to a 100-year-old man in front of all my friends and family. I would never live that down! For years people would be reminding me of how an ancient grandpa beat me at arm wrestling. No way! Not going to happen to this kid. I'd rather wait an entire evening to get my hunting lottery results than suffer that kind of humiliation for years!

CHAPTER 6

LUCKY OR NOT

It was pure misery sitting there, waiting soooo long for my turn. I do have to admit, it was fun seeing the reactions from each person as they got their lottery results. Papa Bruno got drawn for an awesome, rifle buck hunt. He was filled with so much excitement and adrenaline that he took his wheelchair, and rode it around the house pretending that it was a rodeo bull. He waved his cowboy hat in his right hand, high up in the air, and swirled it around. He even yelled, "Yee-haw!" I almost died laughing.

I was super excited for my Aunt Betty! She got drawn for a rifle antelope hunt that she had been wanting to go on for years. She had the first look of relief that I'd seen on her face the whole evening! And I think everyone else was pretty excited they wouldn't have to wait to use the bathroom anymore.

Then it was Jack's turn to go. He stood up from his comfy spot on the couch. It took him a few seconds to stand. He looked tired and worn out. I could tell that he had worked really hard on his farm today. He must have come straight over after work.

Jack had an athletic build. His shoulders were broad and his arms were muscular. His farmer tan showed around his biceps. The contrast in skin color was incredible. His face was soft and friendly. His light blue eyes were piercing, almost like he could look deep into your soul. His teeth were amazingly white. He smiled a lot. I really liked that about him. A lot of the adults I knew rarely had a smile on their face, but that wasn't the case with Jack. It was almost like he smiled so much when he was younger that a permanent smile just stuck.

He walked humbly up to the computer. For someone who had accomplished so much in their life, he sure didn't seem to show any sort of pride. I watched closely as his big, strong hands touched the keyboard. He pecked each bit of information in with his right pointer finger. He had to search for each letter and number. It was obvious that he was not very familiar with the keyboard. Typing in his name, birthdate, and social security number seemed to take forever.

Once all of his information was in, he pecked the return key and submitted his info. He waited patiently as the results loaded. When they came up it was clear that he had not been drawn for anything. His reaction to his disappointing results amazed me. He shared a genuine smile.

He stood up and said, "Well, I guess I won't be hunting any special areas this year, but I'm really excited for all of you that will be. I can't wait to hear all of your hunting stories."

It was so genuine. It was obvious to me that he was truly happy for those that did get drawn. He even made his way over to Papa Bruno and gave him a pat on the back. He congratulated him again on getting drawn for his special buck hunt.

My mom got up and gave Jack a hug and then made her way to the computer. I felt pain in my chest when she saw that she did not get drawn. My heart absolutely broke when Dad didn't get drawn. He tried so hard to play it off like it wasn't a big deal, but I know him. I could see it in his eyes that for some reason this year's rejection hurt more than in years past. I went and gave him a hug. He barely hugged back. I could feel the lack of energy in his embrace.

Finally, after everyone else in the room had received their results, it was my turn. It was late in the evening and pitch-black outside. The rain had picked up a bit, and you could hear it pounding on our metal roof. It had taken hours for my moment to finally arrive. I hopped up out of my chair, and strutted over to the computer. I looked around the room, and every single eye was on me. I whipped out my lucky True Hunter coin from deep inside my front pocket. I looked at it for a second and then gave it a big kiss. Everyone laughed. I chose not to flip the coin into the air, and catch it behind my back. I was too scared I'd end up looking like a fool if I dropped it. I quickly typed in my information. I took a deep breath and searched for the submit button. I clicked it....

CHAPTER 7

LIGHTNING STRIKES

Just as I was about to get my draw results, a terrible flash of light went through the whole house. It was immediately accompanied with a giant KABOOM of thunder. The lights went dark, and the computer screen went blank!

"Noooo!" I yelled out loud. The house was completely dark. I couldn't see anything. We had lost power!

Suddenly, every person in the room was on their feet. Outside there was a loud snapping noise. Then a dancing orange light shone through the window lighting up our living room. We all ran to the big window. I couldn't believe what I was seeing! My family's giant pine tree was on fire! I've never seen anything like it. We rushed out the front door.

A big branch had broken off, and snapped our power lines. Sparks were flying off the telephone pole in every direction. The pine needles on our tree were crackling. The pine cones that were still on the tree turned into small little bombs as they exploded in the heat of the fire. The trunk of the tree was raging with bright blue and yellow streaks of fire. Rain was still coming down hard, but it wasn't enough to put out the blaze.

Dad rushed to the water hose, and sprayed the tree. The flickering glow of the fire soon disappeared. We stood there in awe as we discovered the spiraled evidence of the lightning strike that was left in the tree.

The lightning had struck the tree about 15 feet up the trunk. Bark was missing. There was a massive scar spiraling down the tree like a candy cane. It was a mark that would serve to help us always remember this exact moment of our lives.

I looked over at my dad. He was just shaking his head in awe. We were all soaking wet from the rain, but we didn't care. I don't think anyone standing there had ever seen anything like this in their lives, and they couldn't take their eyes off of the poor, damaged tree.

I looked back inside the house. It was still dark. The lights had not come back on. My mind switched back to thinking about the drawing and finding out if I had gotten drawn for my dream hunt.

I ran over to Dad. He was standing under our covered porch trying to stay out of the rain. I asked, "What now? How do I find out if I got drawn for my hunt?"

He looked back at me and shrugged, "Son, I don't know what to say. I can't do anything about it. We will just have to wait until the electric company fixes the power line."

I tried really hard not to be upset, but I was. That was my moment, and the stupid lightning strike had taken it from me. I looked across the yard to see Jack making his way over to my dad and me. Most everybody else had gotten in their vehicles and gone home. All the excitement was over.

"Now isn't that something to remember. I don't reckon I've ever been that close to a lightning strike!" Jack said enthusiastically.

I looked up at him, and quietly replied, "I guess."

He looked down towards me with kindness and understanding in his eyes. "Oh, I see. You're still wondering whether you got picked for your Devil's Canyon hunt, aren't you?"

I replied, "Yep. I just don't know how long it'll be before I can find out. We have to wait for the electric company to come and fix the stupid power line. Who knows how long that will take. I'm bummed, that's all. Everyone else got their results except for me."

Jack looked over at my dad and said, "Dad, what do you think about you and James coming over to my place real quick? I'm sure I still have electricity at my house. We can use my computer to check James' lottery results. It won't take but a minute."

"Great idea! Let's go!" I blurted out. I ran over to our truck and said, "What are you all waiting for?"

Dad sighed and looked over at Jack with exhaustion in his eyes. "It's been a long, long day, but I don't think I'd ever hear the end of it if I keep James from finding out if he got drawn."

When we got to Jack's place, Jack pulled out his keys and unlocked the front door. We walked in together. His house was empty. It was so quiet. It wasn't anything like the atmosphere over at my house. He took us to his office where his computer was.

I had never been in his office before. He blew the dust off of his keyboard, and let me sit at his desk. I sat down on the cold metal chair in front of the computer. My wet pants made the chair squeak when I sat down.

I looked around the room. There were so many pictures on the wall that I had never seen before, but there was one in particular that caught my eye. It was a picture of Jack when he was a lot younger. He was wearing a brown leather jacket. His hair was greased up, and he was leaning up against an old red Corvette. He looked like he was a Hollywood movie star. In the picture he was standing next to a pretty blonde woman, and he had a baby in his arms dressed in blue. He looked so happy.

"Hmm, I didn't think Jack had any kids," I said to myself.

Just then, Jack spoke and I broke my gaze from the picture.

"Alright young man. Are you ready to see what you got drawn for?"

I turned to the computer and pulled my lucky True Hunter coin back out of my pocket. I looked at it for a few seconds before I put my information into the computer. I rubbed the coin anxiously as I clicked the submit button. Jack's internet was really slow. The government's lottery website was taking forever to load. My heart sank. Was something wrong I wondered, but then the page opened. I looked, and I could not believe what I saw....

I… got… DRAWN!!! It was for the hunt that I wanted most. The archery, bull elk hunt, right in the middle of the rut in… DEVIL'S CANYON!!!! I was in shock. I couldn't even move. Dad picked me up out of the metal chair. He gave me a giant bear hug. He was so excited. "Dad! We're going to get to hunt the Devil's Canyon together again!" I exclaimed.

Jack gave me a big pat on the back and said, "Dang boy, that coin is good luck! I am so excited for you and your dad. That will be a hunt of a lifetime, and you get to experience it at 12 years old. You and your dad are going to make some real memories this year. Just don't try jumping over a tumbling elk again!" he joked.

We all laughed. Life felt perfect.

CHAPTER 8

SUMMER JOBS

Oh my goodness, it was hot. I could not believe how hot it was. Sweat dripped off my forehead and made its way into my eyes. Sweat stings so much when it gets into your eyes! I looked up at the clear blue sky. I didn't see a single cloud. The sun beat down on me relentlessly.

Every day this summer has been hot, but my very last day of work seemed to be the hottest. I'd been doing yard work for a couple of months, trying to make enough money to buy a brand-new bow. My old bow wasn't big enough for me anymore, and it definitely wasn't worthy of a hunt in Devil's Canyon. I'd spent all of my summer break mowing, mulching, weed wacking, and trimming.

A few of my kind neighbors had hired me to do the lawn work that they didn't want to do themselves. They knew I needed to make money for a new bow, and they were awesome enough to provide a way for me to do that.

My last job of the day was weed whacking. It was my least favorite of all the jobs. It's loud, it vibrates my whole body, and it's hard to control. It really wears me out. I decided to take a breather, and I put the weed eater down.

I looked down at my hands. They were rough and callused. My fingertips had small cuts and scratches on them. My hands were so rough they looked like they belonged to a 30-year-old carpenter. I felt a tinge of pride as I looked at them. To me the appearance of my hands represented a summer of hard work. That hard work would turn into a brand-new bow that I would be able to take with me on my bull elk hunt.

A few of the jerk kids in the neighborhood had gotten new bows for Christmas last winter. I was absolutely jealous. Their bows looked so awesome! I admired the sleek shape of the cams at the top and bottom of each bow. Their bows came with sweet sights and fancy rests. The arrows were carbon fiber, and had orange and black veins. Their parents were definitely richer than mine… and they didn't hesitate to rub it in constantly.

"James, what do you think of my new bow? Is it as cool as the new pair of underwear you got for Christmas?" They laughed at me, and then walked away to practice shooting without me.

I came home with tears in my eyes that day because of what those jerks had said. Instead of going out and buying me a new bow my parents sat me down and explained, "Son, if you want a new bow you're going to have to work and make the money yourself. It's that simple. We don't have the money to spare to get you one right now."

The pain in their eyes was real. It matched the pain that was in my heart. I decided at that moment that I would do anything to earn the money for my own bow. Nothing would stop me.

I scoured the internet researching all the different brands of bows. I really wanted a bow that could grow with me. As a 12-year-old I was starting to grow, and knew that if I got a bow made exclusively for a 12-year-old that I would grow out of it too quickly. I found out that the new bow technologies allowed some bows to grow with their owner. I mean, they didn't actually grow, but you could adjust the bow's size by using a little wrench to tighten or loosen the settings.

When I had finally found the perfect bow for me, I printed out a picture of it, and pinned it to my bedroom wall. I wanted to see what I was working for everyday when I woke up, and look at it every night before I went to bed.

My parents told me to picture myself buying the bow. Apparently, if you picture yourself doing something over and over in your head it makes it easier for you to make it happen. I thought it was weird at first, but I got to the point where I could actually see myself shooting this exact bow. It filled me with so much motivation!

CHAPTER 9

DREAM BOW

I had taken the picture of my bow off my wall and put it in my pocket. I called it "my bow" because, even though I don't own it yet, I knew I soon would. My pockets were bursting with the cold hard cash I had made from working all summer.

I finished my weed whacking job. I pulled the picture of my bow out of my pocket and stared. The anticipation was killing me! Dad would be picking me up at any moment to take me to the bow shop.

George, my neighbor, came out and looked at the job I had completed. He smiled and thanked me for all the sweat I had spilled making sure his yard looked terrific. Then he paid me. That was always my favorite part. He reached his hand into his pocket, and pulled out a bunch of 10's. He slowly counted out the money I had earned, and put each crisp 10-dollar bill into my open, callused hand.

He knew I was working hard to make money to buy a bow for my elk hunt. He glanced down and saw the picture in my hand, and asked to see it. I handed him the picture. He grinned, nodded his head, and reached back into his pocket and pulled out a 50-dollar bill.

"You're going to need a good set of broadheads aren't you? How about you use this 50-dollar bill on some of those. Let's just call this a tip for being such a dedicated worker this summer."

Oh man! I was so pumped! I shook his hand and thanked him over and over.

Dad pulled up to the yard, and saw the huge smile on my face. He told me to get in the truck, and off we went to the bow shop. When we got there, I pulled out the picture of the bow I wanted from out of my pocket, and gave it to the shop owner.

He smiled and said, "Boy, you've got good taste! That is a spectacular bow. Your dad must love you a heck of a lot to buy you this one."

I looked up at Dad, and he nodded to me as if to say, "Go ahead and tell him the truth."

So, I did. I said, "My dad does love me a ton, that's for sure. But... I worked every day this summer to make enough money to buy this bow on my own."

I pulled out the giant wad of cash I had in my pocket. It was a little damp from the sweat on my leg. "Sorry it's wet. I know that's gross. I just came from work, and my legs are still a little sweaty."

The owner looked at my dad then at me and replied, "Well young man, I am mightily impressed by your effort. Look at those hands of yours. You can tell that you've worked hard for this. I bet you'll end up being quite the hunter with that type of work ethic."

He told us to hold on a second. He left, and went into the back room. When he came back, he was holding up my dream bow. It was exactly like the picture!

It was midnight black. The riser's pattern was so appealing to me. It was machined in a grid like fashion. The riser connected to parallel limbs. The cams were so big! The red strings connecting the cams gave it some "pop". I was in love. True love.

We set up the bow together. He made some adjustments, and then let me shoot through a paper target to see if everything was tuned right. When you shoot through paper you can see if the arrow is flying straight by what kind of hole the arrow makes. I was amazed at how fast the process was to get it set up. I was even more impressed by how awesome my brand-new bow was!

I had saved up enough to get a nice 5-pin sight, and a fall-away rest. It's cool because with a fall-away rest, there's no friction on your arrow to slow it down at the start of your shot. At least that's what the shop owner told me.

When I went to pick out arrows the shop owner winked at me and said, "The arrows are on me young man. You've really impressed me today. I wish the world had more hard-working boys like you."

He picked out a set of carbon arrows that had the coolest looking black and red veins. He handed them to me. I thanked him with a big two-handed handshake. Then I pulled out the 50-dollar bill my neighbor had given me, and asked him to get me the best set of broadheads he had. I would be hunting in style come September.

CHAPTER 10

THE TRUTH

Every night I went to bed thinking about what it would be like to shoot a giant bull elk with my new bow. Sometimes the excitement of my thoughts made it so I couldn't fall asleep.

Every time that would happen, I'd just lie there in my comfy bed with my eyes wide open. Then with my vivid imagination, I would turn my ceiling into a big movie screen. I would look up and see big bulls bugling and fighting on my ceiling.

I'd watch myself on the big screen make an amazing shot on a giant, proud bull. Then I'd see myself searching for my big bull after I shot him. I would see the joy and absolute excitement on my face when I found him. I'd run up to the bull, and Dad would take an epic picture with his phone. I would hold the antlers far away from my body to make them look even bigger than they actually were.

That always made me smile to myself. Every real hunter knows that trick. After that, I would fall asleep with a big smile on my face.

Imagining that exciting scene always seemed to lead me into amazing hunting dreams. And working so hard in my dreams always made me wake up hungry!

So early one morning, I leaped out of bed with one thing on my mind: Lucky Charms. While I was pouring myself a bowl of those delicious marshmallows for breakfast, Dad came up to me and said, "James, I feel like I should tell you something...."

I cocked my head slightly to the left in response to his odd statement.

Dad continued, "You have never actually been in Devil's Canyon.

"Umm, yes, I have! When I bugled in that bull for–"

Dad interrupted me, "Well you're kind of right. We hunted the Devil's Canyon *area* when we shot that big bull, but you've never taken a step into the actual canyon."

"What are you talking about, Dad? We shot our bull deep in Devil's Canyon. I remember the super steep hill that we sat on when I bugled in our bull," I replied with a little bit of frustration in my voice.

"Let me show you what I mean," Dad said. He opened up Google Earth on the computer and zoomed in on a specific spot.

"Right here is where we parked the day that you bugled in that elk for me."

He pointed to a small clearing on the side of the road.

"And this is the hill we were sitting on when you bugled in our bull."

To my utter disappointment, the hill looked really small, and it was only like 300 hundred yards from where we parked the truck.

"Are you serious, Dad? I swear we walked for miles that morning before we sat down by that big old pine tree."

"Nope. We only walked for maybe 20 minutes. You were having a real tough time. You were only 8 years old, and not nearly as big and strong as you are now. You kept on falling on the slippery rocks, and the deadfall was making it really hard for you to walk. When I saw how much you were struggling, I decided to take you to a good spot that I knew was really close to the road," he stated.

"Son, this is Devil's Canyon...."

He turned on the 3D feature of Google Earth and zoomed out. He rotated the canyon so I could see how steep and scary it actually was. I couldn't believe what I saw.

Devil's Canyon was rightly named! It was beyond steep! It looked like you would need to use a rope to climb down to the bottom. There were rockslides coming off the edges of the canyon, and deadfall was everywhere. In many places there were rock cliffs that went straight down into the canyon floor. Devil's Canyon looked impossible to get down into.

"Not many hunters have ever actually hunted inside Devil's Canyon. The thought of having to climb down there is beyond intimidating," he said.

"The good news is the Devil's Canyon area is huge and there are elk everywhere. If you look over here at this flatter area at the base of the mountain, you'll see some prime hunting ground. It will be a lot easier on our bodies and there are plenty of big bull elk to chase in this spot."

Dad continued, "The Devil's Canyon area holds some of the biggest bull elk in the country, and there is a reason for that. The terrain is difficult even if you don't go down into the actual canyon. Elk disappear into the thick bush at any sign of danger. It is really important for us to make a good plan before attempting to hunt it."

Dad then taught me that it was important to look for three things on Google Earth that would help increase our odds of getting a bull: food, water and bedding ground. The trick was to find all three of those areas in a cluster. If we could find a cluster of feeding, watering, and bedding areas, then we would most likely have a more successful hunt. Together, we found a few of these perfect elk locations, and made a plan of attack.

CHAPTER 11

ROBIN HOOD

To prepare myself for the big hunt I practiced shooting my new bow every day. I got pretty good if you asked me. I was at the point where at 20 yards I could hit the bullseye almost every time. Well, I guess I had never actually gotten all three of my practice arrows in the bullseye at the same time, but I'd gotten 2 in the bullseye lots of times!

I normally shot in the evenings when the sun was about ready to go down. Dad had told me that late evenings were prime time to shoot an elk. So, practicing in low light was important to do, but this day was different. I was shooting in the middle of the day. My dad had his championship softball game early that evening that I really wanted to go to.

Old guys like my dad played softball instead of baseball. I'm not really sure why, but they do. My dad is a rock star when it comes to softball. He's the best player on his team. Actually, I think he's the best player in the whole league!

I decided that before I got ready to go to his game. I'd shoot three more arrows. I pulled my bow back, and held the 20-yard pin right on the bullseye. I slowly pulled the trigger on my release. The arrow made a "Shhhp" sound as it left my bow. It hit the target, and made a "Thud" sound.

"Bullseye. Yes! I love that feeling! Ok, let's do this again," I said to myself.

I took another shot. Shhhp... thud. Another bullseye!

"Oh boy, could today be the day that I finally get three bullseyes in a row?" I whispered to myself.

I put my hand in my pocket, and rubbed my lucky True Hunter coin. I took a deep breath and drew my sweet bow back again. The woven, carbon fiber arrow pulled back slowly across my fall-away rest. "Steady," I told myself. My pin settled on the bullseye. I shot and shhhp... crack!

"What in the world just happened?!" I asked out loud. I was so confused.

The arrow didn't make the "Thud" sound like it always did when it hit the foam target. Instead of a "Thud" sound it made a cracking sound....

I put my bow down carefully, and ran over to the target to see what happened. My jaw dropped as I saw why my arrow sounded so strange. There were still only two arrows touching the bullseye….

My third arrow was stuck inside the first arrow I shot!

"Robin Hood!" I yelled at the top of my lungs.

I shouted so loud that my parents came outside. They looked at me, and asked what was going on. I stepped away from the target, and let them see for themselves.

"James! Are you serious?! Did you just Robin Hood an arrow in the bullseye? How far back were you?" Dad questioned in disbelief.

Mom had a funny look on her face. "Is this a big deal? I don't understand. Looks to me like you ruined an arrow. Aren't those expensive?"

Dad looked at Mom and said, "I've been shooting a bow my whole life, and I've never Robin Hooded an arrow in the bullseye."

I was smiling ear-to-ear. "20 yards, Dad!" I boasted.

Dad took out his phone, and took a picture. He immediately started sharing it with all of his friends.

I stood there in awe. I didn't want this moment to end. I looked closely at the arrow. I saw how the second arrow broke through the nock, and slipped inside the hollow carbon shaft of my other arrow. It went in a quarter of the length of the arrow. The first arrow's carbon weave was ripped apart. It needed to make room for my other arrow. So cool! I carefully took the arrows out of the target making sure that I didn't pull the connected arrows apart from each other.

I went to my bedroom with my parents following me close behind. I grabbed a couple of thumb tacks and put them in the wall above my bed. I laid my "Robin Hood" across the thumbtacks on the wall.

My dad laughed and said, "Now that is a true trophy." He was bursting with pride. I looked at Dad and said, "Are you ready to go hunting in a couple of weeks? Looks like I am!"

CHAPTER 12

CHAMPIONSHIP GAME

"You got this Dad!" I yelled as Dad got up to bat in the bottom of the first inning. He always batted first on his team. He was super fast, and was always so exciting to watch when he got on base. He looked over at me in the stands and winked. I waved to acknowledge that I saw his secret wink to me.

The other team's pitcher lobbed the pitch towards the outside part of the plate. Dad loved those kinds of pitches. He swung expertly, and hit the ball into short right field. For almost any other batter this would just be a single, but not for my dad!

He took off, and cruised around first base without even hesitating. The outfielder picked up the ball cleanly. He looked up, and was surprised to see that Dad was headed towards second base! He threw the ball quickly over to second. Dad dove head first, and touched the base with both hands. He was safe, and it wasn't even close.

Dad stood up and dusted himself off. Everything on him was dirty except for his teeth. He smiled his big white smile as he looked over at Mom and me. His uniform was covered in streaks of clay colored dirt.

His softball team was filled with some local softball legends. There was Jimmy. He was a big dude. Not fast at all, but man could he hit that ball far. He was always hitting home runs. He was the kind of guy where he either hit it over the fence, or popped out trying. I always tried to catch his home runs on the other side of the fence.

There was Johnny. He was their team's super skinny, quirky pitcher. He would do the funniest little wind ups before lobbing the ball over the plate. I thought he looked super silly. He was missing a few teeth. When he smiled, all I could picture in my head was a typical Jack-O-Lantern. I'm thinking he must have taken a few softballs to the face over the years.

Then there was Jack, my baseball coach. He was strong, but rarely ever hit home runs. He would often hit the fence with line drives, and get an easy double out of it. He was always telling me that it's better to hit a line drive than a homer anytime. He wasn't as fast as my dad, but he was still fun to watch. He was super smart, and everyone called him Coach. He batted near the end of the batting order.

This game was intense. You could just feel it in the air. Both teams were intent on winning the championship. Normally there was a lot more joking around on the diamond, but today everyone was being super serious. Every run mattered. Normally, I would run around and play catch with my friends, but not today. I sat right next to my mom, and rooted for Dad's team the whole game.

Just then Dad made an awesome diving catch. He looked like Superman!

I ran over to the dugout, and got my dad's attention. "Dad, that was the most incredible catch I've ever seen!"

He smiled and gave me a fist bump through the fence.

He said, "Well let's see if we can get a couple of runs and bring home the championship trophy. You got your Robin Hood trophy today. It's only fair that I get my championship softball trophy, right?"

By the time we got to the bottom of the last inning, we were losing by one run.

The inning started off with Jimmy. I looked at my mom and said, "Jimmy is going to tie it right now with a homerun bomb. You just watch."

The pitcher let his pitch fly. Jimmy reared back, and took a huge swing. He connected, and the ball flew high into the sky towards the home run fence. It looked like he was going to tie the game right away. The outfielder ran back, climbed the chain link fence, stretched out his glove, and caught the ball. Jimmy was out!

"No, no, no!" I exploded.

I looked over at the dugout, and saw everyone patting Jimmy on the back consoling him. I think he was pretty shocked too. He had his head down, and was shaking it side-to-side in disbelief.

Jack walked up to the plate. We had one out, and were still losing by a run. He took his time. He didn't look nervous at all. The pitcher lobbed the ball in, and Jack just watched it hit the ground behind him. The umpire called it a ball. Jack wasn't about to swing at a bad pitch. He was too smart to do that. He waited and the next pitch was a ball too. Then the next two pitches were balls as well. The pitcher had chosen to not even throw Jack a strike. Jack took his free base and strolled over to first.

I was so confused. Why would they just walk Jack with only one out. Then I figured out what their strategy was. Johnny was up next. He sauntered over to the plate. Johnny was an awesome pitcher, but he wasn't much of a hitter.

He got into the batter's box. He tapped his bat on the plate. He was looking pretty focused. I don't think I've ever seen him so focused.

My dad hollered at him from the on-deck circle, "Johnny, don't hit the ball on the ground!"

Johnny looked over at my dad, and nodded. The pitch came, and he swung upwards at it. He connected, and the ball flew in the air to the outfield. Jack readied himself at first knowing that he could tag up once the ball was caught and then sprint to second base. The outfielder caught the fly ball, and heaved it to second. Jack ran as fast as he could, and dove into second base. It was so close! If the umpire called him out the game would be over.

We all waited on the umpire to make his call. "SAFE!" The umpire yelled. Jack had just barely made it in time. Jack stood up slowly, and flashed his white smile.

He jokingly called over to my dad and said, "You're not the only old man with some speed!"

CHAPTER 13

GAME CHANGER

Oh boy! Two outs, bottom of the last inning, and the tying run on second base. Winner brings home the championship trophy, and guess who was up to bat? My dad! There wasn't any other person I'd want to see batting in this situation.

Since Jack was on second all Dad needed to do was hit a single. That would bring Jack home, and tie the game. All the pressure was sitting squarely on my dad's shoulders right now.

Dad took his time to get to the plate. I could tell that he was trying to decide what he should do. He was a master softball hitter, and could usually hit the ball exactly where he wanted to. He got to the plate. He had this huge smile on his face. I love that he smiled so much, but I don't think the pitcher liked that he was smiling so big. The pitcher returned Dad's smile with a snarl and a grunt.

My heart was beating a thousand times a minute. The suspense was killing me. I wanted Dad to be the hero so badly. I really didn't want him to be the one that got the last out, the one to lose the championship game for his team.

The first pitch came. It was an inside pitch. My dad just let it float by. Strike one! The pitcher kept the angry look on his face. He pitched again. It was also on the inside of the plate. My dad just let it go by. Strike two! My stomach fell. What is he doing? Is he crazy? The stress built in my chest. "Come on Dad! Crush this next pitch!" I yelled loudly.

Dad's smile still beamed on his face. He was taking this stress a lot better than I was! Then the next pitch came. I watched closely to see what Dad would do. While the pitch floated in the air Dad's smile got even bigger!

This was the pitch that he was looking for. It was straight down the middle of the plate. He could hit the ball anywhere he wanted with that kind of pitch. He started to swing. His technique was beautiful! The bat met the softball, and he crushed a line drive to the outfield.

Jack took off from second base. He was easily going to score the tying run. Dad didn't even look to see where the ball was going. He dropped the bat, and took off for first.

My attention turned to that outfielder that caught the ball that Jimmy had hit earlier. He obviously had some major skills. The outfielder ran and dove to try and catch Dad's hit, but he missed! The ball scooted by him, and bounced all the way to the fence.

I looked up. Dad had just touched second base and was on his way to third base. Jack had already scored the game's tying run. Jack was yelling at Dad to stop at third base, but Dad didn't stop! The outfielder got the ball, turned, and threw it with all his might to home plate.

"Man, that guy has a cannon for an arm!" I said nervously.

Dad and the ball were on their way home. Dad's cleats kicked dirt high into the air behind him. It was going to be close! Really close!

Dad started to slide feet first as the catcher held his glove right in front of home plate. The throw was absolutely perfect. The ball looked like it was going to win the race to the plate. It did! It hit the catcher's glove right before Dad's foot got there.

"No!" I couldn't believe it. Dad's foot slid right into the glove. He was going to be out!

But Dad's cleat hit the glove with so much force that the catcher couldn't hold on to the ball! The ball popped out of the catcher's glove! It rolled onto the ground. Dad's cleat caught the edge of home plate. There was a giant snapping sound. The umpire signaled emphatically with his arms outstretched. Dad was safe!!! Dad was safe!!!

"We won!" I yelled at the top of my lungs.

Mom and I stood up and hugged each other in the excitement of the moment.

Dad's team ran out of the dugout, and jumped on my dad who was still lying there at home plate. It was absolute euphoria! I've never seen so many happy old men!

All of a sudden, Jack started to yell, "Get off him! Get off him!"

In all the chaos no one realized that my dad was screaming. He was screaming in pain! The mood changed in an instant. Everyone got off Dad, and backed up to see him grabbing his ankle with both hands. Jimmy looked down at Dad's ankle, turned green in the face, stumbled over to the fence, and puked!

Then I saw what had made Jimmy puke. Dad's foot wasn't where it was supposed to be. The bottom of his cleat was turned towards his face! His ankle was broken! It was broken badly! He must have caught the edge of home plate with his cleat, and the force of his slide snapped his ankle!

Johnny yelled for someone to call for an ambulance, but Dad yelled, "No! Don't call an ambulance! I can't afford an ambulance! Pick me up, and drive me to the Emergency Room!"

Jack and Jimmy picked Dad up. My mom ran to the car and pulled up beside the fence. Dad had tears in his eyes, but it wasn't because of the pain of his broken ankle.

"James' elk hunt. I won't be able to take James on his elk hunt anymore!" He repeated that sentence over and over.

The tears were really flowing. I ran to my dad. I've never seen him cry before.

He looked up at me while being put in the car and said, "James. I'm so sorry. I'm so sorry."

My heart sank. In all the excitement my hunt was the last thing on my mind. But my dad loved me so much that just the thought of missing my elk hunt hurt more than a severely broken ankle.

CHAPTER 14

TOUGH TIMES

I sat in the hospital waiting room with my face in my palms. Dad had been in surgery for hours now. My heart hurt for him. My heart hurt for me. I looked around the waiting room where the whole team had come to support Dad. Jimmy was holding a big championship trophy. At the top of the trophy was a softball player sliding. It was fitting. The championship was won with a slide just like that.

Suddenly, a doctor came out and told us that Dad's surgery was finished. The surgeon had reset Dad's ankle, and put in a titanium plate to support the broken bone. He also said it would be at least 2 months before Dad would be walking on his own again.

The doctor told us that we could go in to see him. He even said the whole team could see

Dad at the same time. We all went in and Jimmy gave Dad the trophy. He said that the team wanted him to keep the trophy since it was his heroics that won them the game. Dad had a big smile on his face.

One by one the players left the hospital room after hugging my dad. It was awesome to see how much they all cared for him. It was like a big family.

My mom looked over at Dad, and she turned to me and said, "Let's go home, and let Dad rest for the night."

I said goodbye to Dad and left the room with Mom, but I noticed that Jack had stayed behind. The ride home was quiet. Mom looked like she was pretty stressed out.

"Mom, are you ok?" I asked.

She started to cry. "Dad's not going to be able to go to work for a while. We were already struggling pretty badly financially. I don't know how we are going to make ends meet. Now with these doctor bills on top of it all. I don't know what to do. I'm sorry, son. I don't want to scare you, but I just don't know what to do. I don't even know how we're going to eat. We didn't want to put any pressure on you to get your elk, but we need that meat more than you realize. But now your dad can't even take you. I don't know what we're going to do."

My heart was broken for her. I didn't realize things were so tough. My parents always had such happy faces. I didn't know they were struggling so much on the inside.

"Mom, I'm sorry. I didn't know. I'm sorry that I won't be able to go hunting to bring home the meat to feed our family this winter," I said with a sniffle.

The silence between us for the rest of the ride home felt so loud. I just didn't know what to do or what to say. I don't think Mom did either.

When we got home, I went to my room. I looked up at my Robin Hood trophy that I put up on my wall earlier that day. I was so ready for this hunt, and now it was over before it even started. I laid down in my bed, put my pillow over my face, and started to cry.

"It's not fair, it's not fair. Why did this have to happen to Dad? Why did this have to happen to me?" I fell asleep with tears running down my face.

CHAPTER 15

NEW PLAN

"Dad! You're home!" I exclaimed loudly. I was still in bed when he knocked on my door and opened it slowly. He was on crutches with a big cast on his right ankle.

"Hey kiddo! Mom told me you were still in bed. How are you feeling?"

"I'm ok. How's your ankle? I asked.

"It hurts, but I'm going to have a sweet scar to remember that slide into home," he chuckled.

"Dad, that was a pretty epic way to win the championship! I'm sorry you got so hurt."

"You know, I've slid like that a thousand times throughout my baseball life. I never thought that breaking my ankle was even a possibility, but sometimes bad things just happen. Mom told me that you two had a bit of a talk on the way home last night. She said it got a little tense."

"Ya... Dad, I'm sorry money is such a problem right now. I didn't realize that things were so bad. I feel horrible that I won't be able to bring home an elk to help feed us this winter," I said softly.

"Well, son, that's kind of what I wanted to talk to you about. What if there was a way that you could go on your elk hunt? It just wouldn't be with me."

"Dad! I won't go without you! This was supposed to be our hunt to go on together. It wouldn't be right to go without you!" I protested.

"James, your mom told you how much we need the elk meat. We are in a really tough spot here. I'm not going to be able to go, but I've found a way for you to go."

Dad stood up, and used his crutches to get to the door. He opened the door slowly....

"Hey James," to my shock, Jack was standing in my doorway.

"You know how you got drawn for the hunt I've been dreaming of going on my whole life? What do you say you help me make my dreams come true, and we go hunt those giant bulls in the Devil's Canyon together?"

My heart leaped! If I was going to go hunting with anyone other than my dad, I would want it to be with Jack. A smile broke through, and I felt hope again. I looked Jack in the eyes and said, "Let's do it!"

The next few weeks were a blur. It was a mix of helping take care of Dad, and getting ready for my hunt. Dad's ankle was still in a lot of pain, and he couldn't move around very well. It seemed like the only time he smiled now was when I was in the room. I got the feeling that he and Mom were having a tough time together. I could hear them arguing in their room over money stuff when they thought I couldn't hear.

This was the first time that I could remember seeing my parents this way. They used to always seem so happy, but now things were different with Dad's broken ankle. Every discussion was about paying the bills or paying the mortgage. At the grocery store mom would put something in the cart that we normally always bought, but then she would look at the price tag and put it back on the shelf. The look of desperation in her eyes almost broke my heart. I decided that the only way to make things better was for me to bring home an elk.

I practiced shooting my bow every chance I got. I didn't want to miss when I got my chance to shoot a bull elk. I practiced all the way out to 40 yards. The joy of shooting was replaced with worrying that I wasn't going to be good enough when the time came to shoot. I didn't want to fail and hurt my family. I felt the weight of the world on my shoulders. I couldn't let my family down.

CHAPTER 16

DRIVING WITH JACK

Jack pulled up to the house driving his beat up, blue truck. It was really old. It looked like he had been driving it his whole life. It was full of dents and scratches from the hood all the way to the back bumper. The engine made a deep rumble sound. It was a lot louder than the newer trucks I had been in. After he parked, he opened the truck door. It squeaked loudly, then he stepped out. I had been waiting for him all morning.

My emotions were all over the place. One second, I was beyond pumped about the hunt, then the next I was terrified that I was going to fail. But really, I was just happy that there was no more waiting. The day finally came to make things happen.

We loaded all of my camping gear. I made sure to grab a sleeping bag and my favorite pillow. My backpack was full of hunting necessities like a canteen, a gutting knife, and a first aid kit. My mom made sure I packed a change of underwear and socks for every day I would be gone. I don't know what it is about my mom and underwear, but it's always the first thing she has me pack.

I grabbed my bow and arrows. Jack suggested that we bring my target too just in case we needed to do some tune up work in the field. You never know what can happen to your sights if you slip and fall.

I went to say goodbye to Mom and Dad. They were both standing by the front door. Dad was leaning on his crutches. I gave them both a big hug and said, "Don't worry. I'll bring home the meat."

Dad got serious and said, "Son, while out hunting you do exactly what Jack asks you to do. OK? He knows the woods. He knows what needs to happen to keep you safe, and to put you in the best position to be successful."

I told him that I promised. I got a little choked up inside. I really didn't want to let my parents down. I turned around and walked towards Jack's truck. I got to the passenger side, and it was locked. I looked over at Jack, and motioned for him to unlock it for me. He leaned over from the driver's side, and pulled up on the round silver knob sticking up out of the door with his strong fingers. I got in and laughed.

"Your truck doesn't have power locks?" I asked.

He smiled back and said, "Boy, the only power in this truck is in the engine. Listen to this bad boy growl."

As he said that he stepped on the gas, and revved up the engine really loud. I laughed. He nodded back with a confident, big smile.

"You got everything you need?" Jack asked before we took off.

"Umm, I think so," I replied.

"Most importantly, do you have your lucky coin?" He asked that question with a serious look on his face.

"Absolutely I do!" I exclaimed as I pulled it out of my pocket. I flipped it over to him. He caught it without taking his eyes off of me.

He looked down at the coin and read the phrase on the heads side out loud, "True Hunter." Then he turned the coin over and read, "Your Legacy." He looked at me with his piercing blue eyes.

"I want you to be thinking about those two phrases while we go on this hunting adventure together. Would you be willing to do that for me?"

"Ya, I can do that," I agreed.

As we drove, I looked at the inside of his truck. It was clean, but worn out. The front seat was a bench seat that had a few worn-out patches where he sat. He drove using a big stick to shift the truck into different gears. He told me that this kind of truck was called a manual, and that he was in control of the gears instead of the truck being in control. I'm not sure why someone would want to do all that extra work, but Jack seemed pretty sold on the idea.

At the top of the gear shift where a black knob would normally be I saw something that made my eyes get big with excitement. There was a baseball! It wasn't a full-sized baseball like we used in little league, it was a little smaller. The leather on the ball had been worn smooth. It wasn't white like a brand-new baseball either. It was brown from Jack rubbing his oily hand on it over the years. He kept his right hand on it while he drove. His first two fingers sat gently across the red seams. He held it the same way I hold my fastball when I pitch. I decided at that moment that I would totally put a baseball on my gear shift if I ever got a truck like his!

Jack didn't talk much while we drove. He kept his eyes on the road mostly. He had the radio on a classic rock station. Every once in a while, he would sing along to the chorus of an old song that I had never heard in my life. Surprisingly, he had a great singing voice.

There was one song I knew and we both sang it together at the top of our lungs. "Bye, bye Miss American Pie, I drove the Chevy to the levy, but the levy was dry...."

He had his window down, and his hair blew in the wind while he sang. He kind of looked like he could be a famous singer. I think that was my favorite moment of the long drive.

CHAPTER 17

MY OLD AIRSTREAM

Jack turned right from the main paved road onto a dirt road. He looked over at me and said, "I talked to a few landowners, and got permission to go through a couple of their gates. I promised to make sure I closed them behind me. This will get us a little deeper into the area than the typical hunter. I came out here earlier this week and set up the camper. That way we wouldn't make any noise setting it up during the hunt. I'm kind of excited for you to see it."

We drove for quite a while on the bumpiest road in the country. I was bouncing around in my seat like a popcorn kernel over an open fire. He had me hop out to open the gates, then he would drive through and I'd have to run and shut them behind us. It was kind of nice to be able to get out of the truck and take a short break from the bumps. He pointed out where the private land stopped and our designated hunting area began. He pulled out an old paper map. It was worn and ripped along the edges. He pointed with his big, callused right finger to show me where we were on the map.

Dad and I had scoured this area using Google Earth, so I had a pretty good idea of where we were. I even surprised Jack a little by telling him about some of the details that I remembered from the 3D view on Google Earth. On his old paper map, he had drawn a star. He told me that the star was where the camper was set up. We were getting really close.

"So, Jack, are there any animals we need to watch out for out here?" I asked.

"No, not really, there will be some coyotes, possibly some bear, and maybe a skunk or two. But if we leave them alone, they will leave us alone," he said.

"Aren't bears big time trouble? I asked.

"Oh, you're thinking about grizzly bears. Ya, grizzlies are the most terrifying animal I've ever seen. I had a grizzly haunt my dreams for years when I was a little guy. Luckily there aren't any grizzlies in this area, just black bears. Black bears are just big cuddly animals. Actually, the last time I saw a black bear he stood up next to a pine tree about his size and started hugging it. He looked like he was dancing with the tree! I yelled at him, 'Go find a pretty bear and dance with her!' He looked at me and ran away. I like to think that he took my advice…."

"That's awesome!" I said.

We drove a little further, and suddenly I saw a shiny metal camper with rounded edges. I shouted, "There it is!"

He said, "Yep! That's my old Airstream. I take her with me whenever I go hunting. She will take good care of us this week."

Jack opened his truck door. It was followed with the now familiar sound of squeaking metal. We hopped out. He opened the Airstream's door.

I stepped inside, and took a look around. I felt like I had jumped back in time. The floor was covered in a strange, green, shaggy-looking carpet. The windows had curtains made out of tie dye fabric. The stove and the fridge were both avocado green. This camper was straight out of the '70s!

"Well, James, what do you think of your home for the next week?"

I told him the truth. "I think it's the coolest thing I've ever seen! Have you had this since the '70s?"

"I sure have! I bought this after I graduated high school. I loved hunting so much as a young man that I basically lived in this thing each fall. Every year I fix it up a little, but I just can't seem to convince myself to change the '70s look that it has."

He had a proud smile on his face. He went over to the fridge and opened it. A bunch of green packets fell out.

"Ya, the fridge doesn't actually work, but I still put our food for the week in there. Have you ever seen one of these before?" He tossed me one of the green plastic packets.

I read the letters on the side of the packet: *M.R.E.*

"What does M.R.E. stand for?" I asked with a confused look on my face.

"Meal, Ready-to-Eat" He said with a grin, "They are from my days in the army. They last forever."

"OK, what do you mean they last forever? How old are these things?" I asked with a turned-up nose.

"Oh, probably 30 years old I'd guess. So only like 18 years older than you are. They are super convenient to have while hunting. Those packets will be our breakfast, lunch and dinner. Would you like to try one for dinner tonight while we go over our game plan for opening morning?"

I gulped. I was kind of hoping he was just kidding with me, but I realized he was being serious.

"Sure, this one says that it is spaghetti. I'll try this one." I was proud of myself for being so brave.

He told me all I had to do was rip open the top of the plastic package. I ripped it open, and three more packets fell to the floor. He told me that one packet was the main course, another was a side dish, and the other was dessert. I opened up the main course half expecting to smell rotting food, but to my surprise it looked and smelled pretty good. He said to add a little bit of water, and stir it up. I did that. I used the little spork (which is a funny looking combination of a spoon and fork) that came with the meal, and took a bite.

"Hey Jack! Not bad! It's not Mom's spaghetti, but it's definitely edible."

"Now try your dessert," he smiled.

I opened the dessert. It was peach cobbler. I gave it a taste, and dang it was pretty good. I was beginning to think that Jack had this hunting thing all figured out. He pulled out the map again, and showed it to me. There were pencil markings all over it. He started to show me what everything meant.

"I've never been drawn for an archery bull hunt in the Devil's Canyon area during the rut, but I've hunted this area plenty in the past. If you look here on the map, I've marked the location of every rub on a tree made by a bull elk that I've ever seen. If you look here, I've marked the wallows that I have found where the elk like to play in the mud. Right here, I have water holes that I've found."

"Holy cow, Jack! You have stuff marked down in the bottom of Devil's Canyon! Have you been down there? Dad told me that very few hunters have ever been brave enough to climb down to the bottom of Devil's Canyon!"

"Yep! I have made the hike to the bottom a few times on hunts in the past. I don't know if I'd ever do it again, it is pretty intense going down. You see these white hairs on my head? They came from the fear I felt on the hike down! But it was pretty amazing down there. It's almost like its own little world."

I was pretty amazed that Jack had gone deep into Devil's Canyon and was still alive to talk about it. I wanted to ask him all about it, but decided now wasn't the time. It was also pretty impressive to see all the hard work, and time that went into making his map.

"So, legal shooting light will begin at 6:30 AM," Jack told me. "So why don't we get up around 5:30 to get an early start on locating some bulls?"

My eyes almost popped out of my head! I couldn't believe it, 5:30 AM! I don't think I've ever gotten up that early in my life, but I wasn't going to complain. Dad told me to do exactly what Jack said so that I'd have the best chance of bringing home a bull. Jack showed me which bed was mine, then he told me to get some sleep.

CHAPTER 18

HELP FROM DAD

The bed wasn't anything to get excited over. I bet it was only a little softer than the ground. The blanket on the bed smelled a little funky. Kind of like it hadn't been washed for a few years. I was pretty happy that I had brought a sleeping bag. I really didn't want to even touch the blanket. Jack turned off the light. The camper went completely dark. I was hoping to fall asleep really fast, so I could get some good rest for the opening morning of my dream hunt.

Jack fell asleep almost instantly. You know how I could tell that he fell asleep instantly? Because the guy snores like a hibernating bear! Oh my heavens! I have never heard such a gosh awful sound! He is such a soft-spoken man when he's awake, but his snoring is anything but soft! I didn't know what to do. There was no escape. I knew I wasn't going to be able to fall asleep with that freight train in the camper.

I grabbed my headlamp and turned it on. I opened up my backpack hoping to find something to muffle his snores. I thought that maybe I could shove some toilet paper in my ears. To my surprise there was a little plastic box with a note taped to it. I grabbed it, and looked closely at the note. It read:

> *Son, I hope you have a tremendous hunt. I believe in you. I really wish I was there with you. It breaks my heart not to be, but I know that you're going to make some amazing memories on this once in a lifetime hunt. I love you, James!*
>
> *Love, Dad*
>
> *P.S. Here are some ear plugs. I'm assuming you will need these… I've camped with Jack the Tyranno**SNORE**aurus Rex many times in the past.*

I laughed out loud. I couldn't believe it. Dad knew this was going to happen! I wonder why he didn't warn me? Maybe he was worried that I'd back out if I knew that Jack sounded like a wounded warthog when he slept!

I put the ear plugs in. Everything went quiet. It was so peaceful. Now that I didn't hear Jack's snoring, my mind was free to drift back to the hunt.

I kind of started freaking out that tomorrow morning I'd get to hunt bull elk, in the rut, in the Devil's Canyon area. It all felt too good to be true. I felt excited, but then I remembered my parents' money situation. I started to feel the pressure of the monumental task laid out before me. I had to bring home the meat, so my family could eat. It bore down on me like a heavy weighted blanket. It made me feel like I couldn't breathe, but finally, luckily, I drifted off to sleep.

CHAPTER 19

OPENING MORNING

"James! James! Wake up!" Jack exclaimed. He hollered loud enough that I heard him through my earplugs. It pulled me out of a pretty amazing hunting dream. I dug out my ear plugs, and opened my eyes to see Jack standing over my bed all dressed in camo.

"Did your dad give you those earplugs?" Jack asked with a questioning look on his face.

"You know everyone tells me that I snore, but I just can't believe–" Just then a bugle interrupted his sentence.

"James, the bulls have been bugling all night. I guess you weren't able to hear them since you were wearing those silly ear plugs. We're in the perfect spot to get in on them quick. Get up and get ready. You've got a bull to shoot!"

I hopped out of bed like I was shot out of a slingshot. My heart started pumping, and adrenaline rushed through my veins. I had laid out my hunting clothes the night before so I was able to change quickly. I was ready to go before Jack was able to get his boots on.

"Let's go!" I said impatiently.

"Alright, alright already. Somebody's a little excited to get started," Jack laughed.

We opened the camper door as quietly as we could. We stepped out onto the tall, wet grass. The dew had already started to soak the ground. The sun was still down. Jack turned on his awesome headlamp that had a red light on it. He told me that elk don't see the red light the same way that they can see a normal white light.

Just then a bull let out a screaming bugle. To me the bull sounded like he was just on the other side of the truck, but Jack said he was actually quite a long way away. I grabbed my bow out of the truck. I looked it over really quick to make sure everything looked right. I had five arrows in the quiver attached to my bow. I wrapped my release around my wrist. I was ready to go harvest an elk!

We started walking quickly towards a nearby meadow. Jack told me that from the bugling sounds he listened to all night, that there was an elk herd in the meadow at the base of the mountain, exactly where Dad and I had planned on hunting. Jack stopped and listened about every ten steps. He checked the wind direction over and over. Luck was on our side, and the wind was blowing directly in our faces.

The sun was coming up slowly. So slowly that I couldn't even tell that it was getting lighter and lighter. Jack pointed to a big boulder.

"That's where we will set up. Maybe we will get lucky, and get a bull to come our direction with a few cow elk calls."

We got to the boulder, and I looked around to see what shooting opportunities I could find. I saw that I had a natural shooting lane set up in front of me. It was the best place to take a shot.

I got on my knees. I had practiced shooting my bow on my knees hundreds of times over the summer for this exact situation. I knocked my arrow onto my bow string, and positioned myself for an easy shot. I was so excited. It wasn't an hour into the first light of the first day, and there were elk everywhere. Through the pine trees I could see the movements of the elk herd. They were grazing. Jack put his cow elk call in his mouth, and made a couple cow calls. To me they sounded like a cross between a cat meow and a bird chirping.

We sat and waited. Then a twig snapped on the back side of my shooting lane, behind a thick row of pine trees. Jack whispered, "Get ready to draw your bow back. Wait until you have a clear shot behind his shoulder before you shoot."

A dark face appeared in the opening where I would have a clear shot. It dropped its head down. It had antlers! But to my disappointment the antlers were not very big. He was just a little spike. He was a young naive bull, and he had just walked into my shooting lane. I didn't hesitate to draw my bow back. I didn't care that the antlers were tiny. I understood that today I was hunting for meat, and this bull was going to feed my family!

CHAPTER 20

HEART BREAK

As I drew my bow back an awful thought snuck into my head.

"What if I mess this up?"

Suddenly, my heart started beating faster. I was struck with worry and anxiety. This simple 20-yard shot seemed to become impossible. I tried to hold my sight steady behind the young bull's shoulder, but I couldn't. My sight was bouncing all over the place. If I missed, I would fail my family, and who knows what would happen to us over the winter. Jack whispered to me, "Calm down and take the shot."

Right then I jerked the trigger on my release. I immediately looked to see where the arrow was going to hit. To my horror, it was way off track. It passed right in front of the unaware bull's nose without even touching him. It continued to fly until it hit a giant rock about 15 yards behind the bull. The sound of the arrow hitting the rock made the bull rear up and jump. He ran crashing through the trees making all the noise he possibly could.

I instinctively started to look at Jack, but turned my face away from him immediately. I couldn't bear to see the look of disappointment that I was sure was on his face. I had epicly failed. My eyes started to well up with tears. I put my face into my arm. I didn't want Jack to see me cry. I failed. I failed my family. I failed at life. I was a failure. I don't know what came over me, but I couldn't stay where I was. I started running in the direction of the camper. I had to get out of this situation somehow.

The tears came fast and hard. I tried to rub the tears from my eyes as I ran as fast as I could. Everything looked blurry. My foot snagged on a tree root that was growing out of the ground. I fell flat on my face. My bow flew out of my hands, and landed on the leaves in front of me. I slid face first across the ground.

I wanted to disappear. I knew that I had failed badly, and the thought of failing killed my soul. I would never be a hunter. Jack would never take me out again. My parents would be so disappointed in me. The neighborhood bullies would all laugh at me. I started to punch the ground in anger. Why did this have to happen to me? Why did I have to get drawn for this stupid hunt? Why did Dad have to break his stupid ankle? Why did I agree to go hunting without my dad?

Suddenly, I felt a hand on my shoulder. It was Jack. He spoke to me softly, but sternly.

"James, calm down. It's ok. You're going to be alright. You'll get another chance. Breathe. It's ok. I'm not upset. It's going to be alright. Look at me. It's ok."

I looked up, and through my tears I focused on his clear, light blue eyes. His face wasn't full of anger, disgust or disappointment like I was sure it would be. It was full of kindness and understanding. My voice choked out, "I failed you. Aren't you disappointed in me?"

"James, listen to me. I'm not disappointed in you at all. I know that you have been feeling a lot of pressure to shoot a bull. You probably feel like life is over. It's not. I've missed my share of bulls. Every hunter misses. The trick is to not let the misses make you miss out on all the amazing hunting experiences you're going to have in the future. Get up. Your hunt isn't over, it's just begun!"

I started to calm down. I thought for sure he would be judging me as the worst hunter the world had ever seen, but instead he was gentle and kind. Seeing his look of compassion filled my heart with hope. The tears stopped, and I was able to think clearly again.

We went back to where I missed, and looked for my arrow. We found it, but the broadhead was bent and the carbon shaft had buckled. The rock had a big chunk missing where the arrow struck. After we finished evaluating the arrow damage, Jack suggested that we go back to the camper to eat. He said that we'd go back out hunting in the afternoon.

CHAPTER 21

LOOKY LOOS

Once we got to the camper, we had some M.R.E. pancakes. They weren't very yummy. They were rubbery and tough. They kind of tasted like they were 30 years old.

After I forced down the less than desirable pancakes, I asked Jack if I could go out on a short walk alone to think about my experience from the morning hunt.

He nodded and said, "That's a great idea. How about you take your coin with you?"

As I walked, I pulled out my True Hunter coin. I ran my fingers over its edge. I shined it up a little and then studied it. "True Hunter"... I didn't feel like a true hunter right now. What's the opposite of true? Fake. I felt like a fake hunter.

I flipped the coin over. I noticed how the older person had his hand on the younger person's shoulder. I remembered how Jack had put his hand on my shoulder earlier this morning to help calm me down.

"Your Legacy" the words on the coin declared. Jack definitely had a legacy. Everyone knew that he was a great man. His legacy grew even more in my eyes after the way he treated me this morning. I hoped I could be like him when I grew up.

As I looked at the coin it was as if it began to speak to me. "James, what is *your* legacy going to look like?"

I thought about that idea. I absolutely didn't want my legacy to be that I was a failure.

The coin seemed to respond, "You're only a failure if you choose to quit."

That thought hit me hard. I had a choice to make. I could either quit and go home, or I could try again. I felt my chest swell and fill with a new sense of determination. I was not going to let that moment when I missed the spike define who I was.

"I am not a quitter," I said out loud.

I could still succeed or at least give it everything I had until I was out of time. That's what Jack would do.

I made my way back to camp. I grabbed my bow, and made sure that it wasn't damaged after my fall earlier that morning. Thankfully, it looked pretty good. The strings were not frayed, and there wasn't any damage to the riser, limbs or cams. I'm so glad it landed on soft leaves.

I grabbed the target that Jack had told me to bring along in case I needed to do a tune up. I set it up, and recreated the 20-yard shot that I missed. I got on my knees, and pretended that a spike was walking in. I drew back, and let the arrow fly. The arrow hit the center of the bullseye.

"How is that possible?" I said out loud. I missed the spike by more than 3 feet. I figured my sight had been bumped or something else was wrong with my bow to miss that badly.

Jack walked up behind me. "Nice shot, kiddo!"

I turned to him, and put my hands up in the air to show my confusion.

"How did I miss so badly?" I asked humbly.

He nodded and said, "You had a bad case of what I call the Looky Loos."

"The Looky Whattys?" I asked with a laugh.

"The Looky Loos," he repeated.

"The moment you pulled the trigger on your release, you jerked the bow to the right to try to get a clear view of where your arrow was going to go. When you did that, it threw your arrow off course. You need to focus on your follow through. Let the arrow come off your bow straight, and you'll do what you just did to that target," he declared.

"Jack, have you ever had the Looky Loos?" I asked.

"As a matter of fact, I have. I believe it was my first shot at an animal with my bow. It was a young buck, and I was even closer than you were to that spike. I completely missed to the right. Did exactly what you did, actually. I'm pretty sure most excited new bow hunters do it to some degree."

This was news to me. I didn't even know the Looky Loos were a thing.

"Well, I'm never going to do that again," I declared.

I shot a few more times, and got my confidence back.

I looked at Jack and said, "I'm sorry for the way that I reacted today. I am ready to try again. If that's ok with you?"

CHAPTER 22

BULL STRATEGY

That evening's hunt wasn't very productive. We walked a ton, and heard a lot of bugling elk. But they were far away, and there was no way that we were going to get to them before dark.

As we walked back to the camper in the darkness Jack and I came up with a game plan. In the morning we would get up earlier than we did today, and plan to stay out the whole day. If we did that, then we could cover more ground and maybe get another chance at a bull.

We woke up early that next morning and worked our tails off chasing bugles all that next day. Actually, we kept to this method for the next 4 days. We would get up early, and take a day's worth of MREs with us. We hiked, and hiked, and hiked some more, following bugles that always seemed to go silent once we got closer. It was exhausting and frustrating and exciting all at the same time. Each day that passed meant I had one day less to get my bull. After my crying episode, I tried so hard to not get down on myself for messing up. But what if that spike was my only chance at a bull this whole hunt?

I learned so much from Jack every day we spent together in the field. Jack's main goal was to get me in a position to get a bull. He did almost all of the bugling. We would locate and focus on a bugling bull. Then we would try to convince the bull to come to us by pretending to be another bull. Bull elk are super territorial, so when they hear another bull elk nearby, they feel the urge to fight.

Jack would set me up at what he called a "pinch point" or a "funnel". For example, a spot where a wall of thick deadfall and brush would guide an elk to where I was waiting.

The plan was that I would get on my knees, and get ready to shoot. Jack would silently make his way to another spot behind me. We would end up probably 100 yards away from each other.

His job was to bugle at the bulls and keep their attention on him, behind me. The idea was that the bulls would walk to where he was bugling, searching for the "challenging bull".

The hope was that the bull would have a good idea where Jack was, but wouldn't have a clue that I was waiting in between for a clean shot.

Jack was really good at bugling. He sounded just like a real bull. Sometimes to get the bulls really mad he would grab a dead tree branch, and thrash it against a live tree. He did this to imitate the sound of a real bull raking his antlers on a tree. I had to remind myself that I was hearing Jack a few times, since he sounded so much like a real bull. My heart leaped every time I heard him bugle!

The hard part of what we were doing was playing the wind just right. The incoming bulls would circle around to try to get our scent. They wanted to make sure they were coming into a real elk and not a hunter. I decided that elk are extremely smart, and good at staying alive.

CHAPTER 23

I STINK

We got close a couple of times, but never close enough for a clean ethical shot. My admiration for Jack grew over those 4 days. He worked so hard to help me accomplish my goal of harvesting a bull elk. He was so selfless. His old body was having to endure days of hard hiking all in the name of serving me. I pulled my lucky coin out while we rested for a few minutes. I read the "True Hunter" words on the face of the coin again.

Spending time with Jack helped me better understand what that phrase meant. Jack was being a true hunter, and he didn't even have an elk tag. He was teaching and sharing his knowledge with me. He was sacrificing his time and energy just to help me (and my family). He was so understanding of my emotions and frustrations. He showed me love and kindness.

I looked at the coin again, and studied how the big buck was jumping out of a compass. The compass must stand for doing things the right way. I noticed how much admiration and respect Jack showed these beautiful creatures. He wasn't all about blood and gore that you sometimes see in the ads of hunting magazines. He was more interested in the experience, and the challenge of helping me harvest one of these magnificent animals. I put the coin back in my pocket.

The fifth day in the woods had been especially hard. We didn't hear a bugle all day. My legs and feet were aching pretty badly. My shoulders hurt from carrying my heavy pack. We had been climbing over deadfall all day. Deadfall was the worst. I hated it. I swear we walked 15 miles trying to find some action. It was so discouraging doing so much work without even hearing a bugle. I looked over at Jack and he just shrugged his shoulders. "Some days in the elk woods are just pure work," he said. I nodded in agreement. I was too tired to even open my mouth to reply.

It was getting dark and Jack stood up and said, "Well, let's get back to the camper, and get a good night's rest before we try again tomorrow."

We started hiking again. It wasn't too long into the hike back to the camper that I realized that I needed to "go" if you know what I mean.

"Hey Jack, nature is calling. I'll be right back!" I whispered loudly.

I went off to the right and found a nice, big tree to water. As I got to the tree, I saw something black scurry under a bush near the tree.

I turned my red headlamp on. This was the first animal I had seen all day, and I was super curious to find out what it was. It was bigger than a squirrel, but it wasn't big enough to scare me in any way. I grabbed a big stick, and shoved it into the bush over and over. I was hoping to scare the animal out of the bush so I could see it, but it didn't flee. I moved a branch of the bush to the side with my stick.

Suddenly, to my absolute horror, I saw the backside of a black and white critter. I watched as if it were in slow motion, as the terrified skunk lifted its white streaked tail. Before I could retreat from my position, I watched the skunk release its smelly defense all over me….

"Ahhhhhh!" I yelled.

"It's in my mouth! It's all over me! Gross! Gross! Nooooo! Are you serious!?" I sputtered out of my skunkified mouth.

Jack ran over to where I was hunched over spitting, trying to get the liquid stink out of my mouth. The stench reached his nose quickly, and he figured out exactly what had happened.

"James! Did a skunk just spray you?" he hollered with a laugh.

I turned to him with my mouth wide open. I spit again trying to get the awful taste out of my mouth. I still had the stick in my hand.

"Whoa kiddo, you stink super bad! You didn't poke a skunk with that stick... did you?" Jack asked, shocked.

"Umm... I might have poked a skunk with this stick," I muttered with embarrassment.

"I can't believe that just happened!" I yelled again.

Jack fell on the ground and started laughing. "In all my years of hunting I have never seen this happen. Oh, James. I'm sorry! I can't believe you got sprayed by a skunk! Why in Heaven's creations would you poke a skunk with a stick?"

I felt myself start to get mad, but then I stopped. I realized that it would be easy to show my anger, but that wouldn't change anything. Instead of getting mad, I chose to laugh.

I said through my laughter, "Oh man! I stink! I can't believe I just did that! My parents won't ever let me back into the house smelling like this!"

Jack got up off the forest floor and exclaimed, "Well, kiddo, you better believe you won't be sleeping in my Airstream tonight! I have a strict 'No skunk stink policy'. And boy, you stink!"

We laughed all the way back to the camper. He told me there really wasn't anything we could do about the smell way out here in the woods. We would just have to endure the smell together. On the bright side, Jack said that the skunk smell was a great cover sent to hide my stinky human smell. The elk would smell skunk instead of me!

Jack came out of his camper with an old hammock and threw it at me. "Go set up your bed for the night. That hammock is old, and needs to be burned anyway," he said jokingly.

I took the hammock and set it up. "At least it's a nice night," I said with a half-smile.

A few minutes later Jack popped out of his camper and made his way over to me. He had a red, paisley bandana over his nose like an old western outlaw. I think he was trying to protect his nose from my stench.

"James, I had a thought come into my mind today…" he paused for a moment.

"Actually, I can't stop thinking about it. I've been trying not to think about it all day. I don't want to think about it. But I just can't shake the thought," he said with a solemn tone in his voice.

"It's Devil's Canyon… it's almost like it's calling to me… calling me to hike deep down to the bottom of it," he said as his voice trailed off.

"Oh wow! You are thinking about taking us down the actual Devil's Canyon? How would we do that? Is there even a safe way down? I know you've been down it before. How did you do it?" I asked my mind full of questions.

Jack looked at me with a glimmer in his eyes.

"There is a secret way down. I found it years ago. It's a well-hidden game trail. It's the way the animals use to get from the top to the bottom. It's still super difficult, and if we attempt this you may even get a couple of white hairs on your head!" he smirked.

"Let's do it! Dad always says 'Go big or go home'. I want to go big!" I said with an adventurous smile.

"We only have 2 days left to hunt before it's time to take you back to your parents. I say we sleep down in the canyon tomorrow night. We will have to bring our packs anyway in case you shoot something down there," he explained.

"I bet you there is a monster bull deep in that canyon," I said with excitement.

"James, there has to be!" Jack replied with a new found energy.

So, before we turned in for the night Jack threw all of my gear out of his camper so I could pack it in my pack. He wasn't going to let me take a step into his precious Airstream smelling the way I did.

I couldn't believe what we were about to do. In the morning I would join the ranks of the few brave hunters who had ever hiked to the bottom of Devil's Canyon.

I slept well that night in that old crusty hammock. Although, if I had known what awaited me at the bottom of Devil's Canyon, there's no way I would have ever fallen asleep....

CHAPTER 24

GENIUS ELK

The next morning, I woke up at 3 AM. I hopped out of the hammock ready to take on Devil's Canyon. I made my way over to the camper. I could hear that Jack was still asleep, and still snoring like a hippo with allergies.

"Seriously though, how is it possible for a human to make that kind of noise?" I muttered under my breath.

I opened the camper door, and it squeaked as loud as Jack's snoring. I took one step inside and Jack hopped out of bed, throwing his fist into the air like he was under attack!

"Jack! It's just me, James. Can't you smell me?" I called out.

He wiped the sleepies out of his eyes, laughed, and said, "You can't scare an old army man like that! I could have hurt you! But you're right. You still stink to high heavens. Get out of my camper!"

I practically jumped outside as I heard Jack grumble, "No skunk smell in my camper. I have one rule, just one rule!"

Jack got ready really quick. We grabbed our overnight packs and headed towards Devil's Canyon. It wasn't long before we heard a deep ear-shattering bugle. It was far, but man was that a powerful sound. Jack pulled out his map to give us an idea of where it came from.

"It looks to me like that bugle came from down deep in Devil's Canyon a couple miles from here. Are you sure you're up for the hardest hike you will ever go on? What do you think, James? Should we chase what could be a monster bull down there?" asked Jack.

"Are you serious? Of course we should chase him! I'm up for the hike of a lifetime. I really, really want to see what kind of bull made that scream," I replied.

"Scream?" Jack scoffed, "You mean beautiful melodious music." He tried to say that with a straight face, but a smile broke through.

So, Jack took us to the secret trail that led down Devil's Canyon. We had to push through super thick brush just to get to the beginning of the trail.

Before we started down Jack looked at me and said, "Above all else you have to be as careful as possible. Take your time. Don't do anything stupid."

I nodded in agreement and said with a smirk on my face, "Don't do anything stupid. Got it."

Then we took our first steps downward. The terrain was rocky and steep. It was really hard to keep my balance with my heavy backpack and bow. I was trying so hard not to fall and hit my bow on the rocks. That would be a disaster. I followed the exact path that Jack took. Step for step.

He was like a mountain goat. He traversed the terrain swiftly and carefully at the same time. Watching Jack reminded me of my dad hiking the day I bugled in that bull for him. He was so nimble and quick on the rocks and logs. I missed Dad like crazy right now.

As we worked our way down the canyon, my legs started to get really tired. This was extremely hard work. My ankles started to feel the pains of steep, awkward hiking. A blister formed quickly on the outside edge of my big toe on my left foot. It throbbed with each step.

I know people say going uphill is harder, but going downhill sure hurts my knees. Every step I took felt like I was fighting gravity from pulling me down the fast way to the bottom of the canyon. I could just imagine what Jack was feeling. He wasn't as young as he used to be. At least that's what he kept telling me.

Suddenly, an explosive bugle echoed off the canyon walls. My heart started to pound hard. I looked over at Jack and he looked at me with big eyes.

"That's a big bull for sure!" he said.

After hearing that, I didn't feel tired at all anymore. I was practically jumping up and down with excitement! He pulled the map out again, and tried to figure out where the bugle may have come from.

"I bet you they are down in this open area about a mile away from us. They are most likely still feeding. Elk love to feed down low at night and into the early morning. Then they will usually work their way up the canyon to bed after the sun rises and it gets warmer," he explained.

"We have to pay attention to the thermals down here," he said.

"Thermals? You mean like underwear?" I asked.

"No, no. Not underwear. Thermals are how the air moves in steep locations. You know how hot air rises?"

"Sure, I learned that at school," I said.

"Well in the heat of the day the air warms up. Then the air moves upwards to the tops of the hills, or in our case towards the top of the canyon. When the day comes to an end, and the sun begins to go down, the air starts to cool off. When that happens the air switches direction, and the cooler, heavier air goes downhill.

The elk use these thermals to coordinate their movements. During the day time they are usually bedded up higher so that the air can bring any scent of danger from below up to them. Then before the air changes direction they begin to walk downhill with the wind in their faces towards a feeding area. Once they get to the feeding area the sun goes down and then the thermals switch. The wind starts coming down off the canyon walls bringing any scent from above them to their sensitive noses."

"Holy moly, elk are seriously geniuses! No wonder they are so hard to get close to!" I exclaimed.

Jack was so smart. I was really thankful that he was doing this with me.

"OK, so what should we do? It's almost daylight," I asked.

"Well, I say we try to get our eyes on them before they head up to bed. I don't think we will have time to make much of a move on them this morning. The heavy cool air is coming down off the canyon walls right now. Can you feel it?"

"Yes! I totally can. So we can't get above them or they will smell us," I stated.

"Exactly! So, let's try to get to the bottom of this canyon first before we work our way to the meadow where they are most likely feeding. We need to be on the same level that they are on," he explained.

We started hiking with purpose. We were moving really well until we hit a really steep spot. My legs started to shake as I looked at the drop below us.

"Let me take your bow during this part of the hike. I promise I will keep it safe. You need to use both of your hands to hold onto the tiny aspen trees growing out of the rocks so you don't go rolling down this ravine. This is the toughest part of the hike. Once we pass this it will be much easier," he explained. "Please don't die," he quickly added as he turned to make his way down.

I started to follow. Sweat began to bead up on my forehead. My heart was inching closer to panic mode. My feet were slipping on the tiny rocks below them. I turned around and got down on my knees and held on to the tiny aspen trees for dear life. I went down backwards. I let my feet slide under me until I was on my belly. Then I grabbed a sapling and scooted further down. I looked down and saw Jack standing on a flatter piece of ground waiting to catch me if I fell.

Just then the loudest noise I've ever heard burst out of a bush a few yards away from me. It scared me so bad that I let go of the branch that was keeping me safe. I started sliding quickly down the steep ravine. My stomach scraped along the sharp rocks as I slid. I thought this was the end of me. My hands grasped at the loose rocks as I slid. I was gaining speed. I closed my eyes and clenched my teeth. I braced myself for the long fall off the cliff's edge.

Thankfully, as I passed by Jack, he grabbed my backpack and stopped me from sliding to my death. I scrambled to my feet with panic in my eyes.

"What was that?!? What made that terrifying noise?" I demanded.

Jack tried not to laugh and said, "That was a grouse. A big dumb bird. They have been giving elk hunters heart attacks since the beginning of time. When they take off, they beat their wings really hard and it makes that terrible sound."

"A bird made that noise?"

I couldn't believe it. I almost died because of a stupid bird. My heart was still beating a thousand times a minute.

I looked at Jack and stated, "That is no ordinary bird. That is a **demon** bird, sent straight from the mouth of Devil's Canyon to terrify us!"

"You know, I can agree with you on that one. I hate grouse," Jack said with a snarl.

"Thanks for saving me. My parents would have killed me if I died!" I joked.

After I got my heartbeat under control, I lifted up my shirt. It looked like a grizzly had taken a swipe at my stomach. The sharp rocks had left their mark. I opened my first aid kit and found an antibacterial ointment. I applied it generously to the deep scratches on my body. After I took care of my wounds we got back to hunting. We spotted the perfect place to stop and find the bugling bull through our binoculars.

The sun started peeking over the canyon walls. We didn't have much time to hike the mile that was in front of us. Every now and again the big bull would bugle. We could tell we were getting closer by how much more intense the bugle got.

Once we got a couple hundred yards from the meadow, we double checked the wind. It was coming from left to right. That was a good thing. The elk were directly in front of us. Jack pointed to a higher point downwind from the elk and said we needed to get there fast. When we got to our spot, we pulled out our binoculars. I immediately started looking for the herd bull. Through the binoculars I could see cow elk everywhere.

Just then the king of the elk appeared....

CHAPTER 25

THE KING

He was magnificent! His antlers ran all the way to his rump. As he turned his head the white tips of his back tines scratched his hind quarters. His body was muscular. Every step he took made his shoulder muscles bulge. I counted the tines on the left side of his rack 1, 2, 3, 4, 5, 6, 7, 8! Then I counted the tines on the right side of his rack 1, 2, 3, 4, 5, 6, 7, 8!

I looked at Jack and I whispered, "Do you see him? He's an 8x8! He's an absolute monster!"

"What?! Where is he? I still haven't found him!" he whispered back. I started to point, but at that exact moment the king herd bull bugled again. Jack looked through his binoculars and found him. He looked at me with excitement in his eyes.

"James, I don't know if I've ever seen a bull that big! That's what you call a Monarch! He's something special!"

We both sat there in complete awe of this magnificent animal. He held his head high, and walked with purpose and strength.

He was the king of the elk, and he knew it. Every elk in that meadow knew it. I stared at him through the binoculars. I watched every move he made with absolute wonder. When he bugled, his belly bounced up and down as he made the different sounds of his royal call.

The king put his head down, and pushed a cow elk out of his way. At that very moment, another tremendously powerful bugle erupted from the other side of the meadow. The king jerked his head up as if he had just been insulted....

The king stamped his feet. He raked his enormous rack on a nearby shrub. Then he stretched his neck out, and let out a blood-curdling bugle. This bugle was different from the ones we had heard earlier. This was meant to be a warning. I looked through my binoculars to find where the other bugle had come from.

I couldn't find him. I looked over at Jack. He was glued to his binoculars. He wasn't about to miss a second of this challenge.

"Jack, where is that second bugle coming from?" I asked.

Jack lifted his index finger and pointed without putting his binoculars down. I searched in the direction that he pointed. Just then, the challenger bugled again. It was a fierce bugle. I looked in the direction that the bugle came from.

There he was. I won't ever forget the moment when I first saw the challenger. He was running with his head down low. He was charging the king! The king reared up, jumped forward, lowered his head, and charged towards the challenger.

Their antlers met with a thunderous clap. The sound echoed off the canyon walls. The king bull pushed with all his might and pushed the challenger backwards.

The king's massive shoulder muscles were bulging with each movement that he made. But the challenger wasn't about to be pushed around. He lowered his head nearly to the ground, and lifted with his swollen neck. The king lost his front footing as the challenger bull pushed him to the side. The king disengaged his antlers momentarily as he regained his footing. He then leaped towards the challenger with his powerful back legs. His antlers crashed into the challenger's thick rack. Both sets of antlers clicked and clacked as each bull bullied and jockied for the superior position.

I tried to count the points on the challenger's rack, but it was impossible to do with their antlers tangled together. His antlers were a darker brown than the king bull, almost a dark chocolate color. The tips of his tines were bone white. He was younger, but every bit as strong as the king. But what drew me to the challenger the most were his eyes. The fur around his eyes was white. His eyes were a deep, intense black. But it wasn't the color that consumed me, it was the look of pure determination that I saw in them. This challenger had made his mind up that he was going to defeat the monarch king.

The epic fight continued as their hooves tore up the meadow's grass. Sweat rolled off of each of their backs. The challenger dug down deep, and pushed the king back again. The king disengaged again, and took a few steps to the side.

Then without warning the magnificent king charged the challenger. He caught the challenger off guard. The challenger wasn't properly squared up to take the king's tremendous force. The challenger's body crumpled, and he fell to the ground. The king showed no mercy. He hit the challenger again while he was on the ground trying to get up.

That last hit caused a flight reaction from the challenger. He got up and ran away. The king stretched out his sweaty neck. He bugled a victorious message to all the elk in that canyon that he was and always would be **The King**.

The challenger continued to run and crossed about 80 yards in front of us. After he passed us, he ran up the canyon wall, crashing through the difficult canyon terrain. Branches snapped and crashed as his enormous rack broke through the thick brush. The sounds he made as he ran did not sound like they came from a defeated bull. They came from a bull determined to make a comeback.

CHAPTER 26

ELK FEVER

"James, I hope you never forget what you just saw. I've hunted my whole life, and have never seen such a battle of wills. Those are two of the biggest bulls I have ever seen. We could go home right now, and I'd be happy reliving this memory for the rest of my life!" declared Jack.

My heart was beating out of my chest. The adrenaline was coursing through my veins. I was now completely and utterly addicted to elk hunting. The bugles, the fight, the determination I saw in these majestic creatures created a swell of total admiration for these royals of the forest. I realized now that hunting was more about the hunt than the kill. The experience of being in these woods with these animals was a wonderful gift.

"Do you want to go after the challenger bull?" asked Jack.

He continued, "I think we might have a chance to get to him right now. He's upset and isn't playing the thermal game correctly right now. The wind is still coming down off the canyon walls. He went up. He won't be able to smell us if we hurry up, and chase him up the canyon. I doubt he went too far."

Without even thinking I said, "Let's go!"

My adrenaline was through the roof. I could sprint up that canyon right now. I grabbed my bow. Jack said that we should leave our packs on the ground, and come back for them later that night.

"It will make it easier for us to get up the canyon quickly," he explained.

I dropped my bag and we headed up the canyon. We followed the beaten path that the challenger bull had made. It was pretty easy to follow. He had left a trail of total destruction in his path. We looked up ahead of us on the trail. There was a thicker patch of trees and bushes. It looked like he had just crashed straight through them.

We hurried upwards, and got to the edge of the thick patch, and took a quick break. Jack was breathing pretty hard from the quick ascent up the canyon walls. Suddenly, a monstrous bugle came from the other side of the super thick patch. I had heard that bugle before. It was the challenger for sure.

The bugle was earth-shatteringly loud. It sounded like we were right on top of him. After his bugle he started thrashing his antlers in the trees. He was making a racket beating up some poor tree. Stomping sounds came next. He was pounding the ground with his hooves. There was silence for a few seconds, and then the thick trees right in front of us started shaking violently. The bull was raking with all his might.

My heart started pounding again. I felt energy shoot through my body. Then he bugled right at us. We were so close that I could smell his breath. He couldn't have been more than 5 yards away from us. The thick cover made it so we couldn't see him, but oh was he there. The bugle made every hair on my body stand straight up. I looked down at my hands, and they were shaking uncontrollably. I didn't know what was wrong with me. I shakily grabbed an arrow, and knocked it on my new bow.

Jack tapped my shoulder and pointed to an opening to the right of the thick brush. I turned my body to set up for a shot on this angry, determined bull. I watched the trees shake as the bull made his way into the clearing. The challenger slowly began to appear in the opening.

His face appeared first. He was walking straight into my shooting lane. I could see the white fur around his eyes. In fact, I could see each individual hair around his pitch-black eyes. He was so close I could almost reach out and touch him. He took another step, and his antlers appeared. The bases of his antlers had to be as thick as a baseball bat. His eye guards were at least 14 inches long. Then he took one more step. His whole body was right in front of us. His antlers reached to the back of his hind quarters. I could see the color change from his tan body to his dark head. Then he bugled....

Never in my life would I see or hear this again. A true monster bull bugling 10 yards away from me. I saw how his mouth opened. I saw how his lips curled, and how his stomach heaved as he sounded off towards the canyon floor. His bugle told the whole canyon that he wasn't defeated, but that he would be back to challenge for the throne.

I tried to draw my bow back, but I had lost all control of my limbs. I was shaking uncontrollably. I shook so hard that my carbon arrow started bouncing up and down, as if it were tap dancing, on my drop away rest. The sound of my arrow's dance made its way directly into the challenger's ear. The imperial giant looked directly at me. There was a moment when our eyes met, and we both stared deep into the other's soul. Then he snorted violently, turned, and leaped back into the thick cover thrashing as he made his escape.

I looked over at Jack. He was shaking uncontrollably as well. We sat there together shaking for a few moments before he spoke reverently, "I haven't had elk fever in 20 years."

"What's elk fever?" I asked with a shaky voice.

"The uncontrollable shakes that both of us just had. That is elk fever. There is nothing like it in the world."

He reached out his arms, and gave me a hug. We were both still shaking. Then he said to me, "Thank you for letting me be a part of your elk hunt. I will never forget this experience that I am having with you. Being out here with you has filled some big holes that I have in my life. Thank you, James."

We both let go and stood up. We started reliving what we had just experienced together.

"What just happened? How in the world did we get so close to that bull?" I asked.

"You know, I'm thinking it's the skunk scent that you decided to bathe in last night! I don't think he was able to smell us past your pungent stench!" He laughed as he said that last part.

We walked around to the thicket where the bull had been thrashing. It was really torn up. It was incredible how much damage he was able to make in such a short amount of time. There was a tree, at least 8 inches thick in diameter, where he had completely stripped the bark off.

"It's almost like he was training to take another shot at the king," Jack said.

"I looked straight into that bull's eyes, and they were full of determination. That bull is not going to give up just because he failed once. I don't think it's in his nature. He's going to get back up, and fight the king bull again. Mark my words. He's not going to give up!" I declared.

CHAPTER 27

EPIC REMATCH

"Who knows where the challenger ran off to. We probably won't ever see him again. Let's get to a high point, and see if we can locate the king. The thermals are still coming down the mountain. I bet you they start working their way up the north face of the canyon really soon," said Jack.

We got up to a good vantage point on the south side of the canyon. Then we watched through our binoculars to see where the king would take his herd of cows. As I looked through my binoculars, I found the king bull. He was so regal. It was almost like he was born to be a king. He held his head high, and walked like he was truly royalty. Then, just like Jack predicted, they all started making their way up the north side of the canyon.

"How did you know they would go up the north side?" I asked Jack.

"These September days still get pretty warm. The elk like to stay cool, and the north facing side of the canyon will stay cooler than the south side. The sun won't hit it directly," replied Jack.

"That's right. Dad told me that when we were looking at Google Earth together," I remembered aloud.

We watched as the elk found thick cover on the north side of the canyon and proceeded to lay down.

"Do you feel that?" asked Jack.

"What do you mean?" I responded.

"The thermals have switched. Do you feel the warm air moving upwards now?"

"As a matter of fact, I do! You weren't kidding about how the air would switch once the sun got high enough. The elk timed their bed time almost perfectly, didn't they?" I said.

"They are really smart animals. I respect them so much," said Jack.

Jack and I discussed our game plan for the evening hunt. We knew where they were bedded down, and where they would most likely be headed in the evening. We just had to figure out when and where we should set up to give us the best shot at the king. We pulled out the map. As we looked at the map together, I realized that we hadn't seen the elk go to water yet.

"Jack, do you think they will go to a water source before they go back to the meadow to feed? They've got to be thirsty, right?

"James, what a great idea! I love the way you're thinking."

The map showed two different water sources that they could potentially go to. One was smaller but higher up near the meadow, and the other was bigger and a bit lower than the meadow. We had to choose which water source made the most sense. After some deliberation we chose the pond lower than the meadow. It was bigger, and in our opinion felt like it made more sense for a herd to go to. It was definitely a gamble. If we chose wrong, we wouldn't have a chance at getting close to the king this evening.

We started making our way to the lower water source. We stayed on the south side of the canyon to avoid having our scent go up with the thermals on the north side where they had bedded down.

It was quite the hike. There was deadfall everywhere. It was like a giant windstorm had swept through the canyon. The trees had been violently ripped out of the ground. We had to navigate the steep terrain and the deadfall. It was exhausting. My legs were so tired from the morning hike. Every time I had to climb a dead tree it made me want to sit down and take a long break. But we felt good about our decision and pushed forward with the hope that the king would reveal himself again that evening.

We found the pond and it was covered in elk tracks. What made it even better was there was a spot above the pond where we could watch the meadow with our binoculars, and scout the movements of the elk. The sun started to make its way down and shadows began forming in the canyon. The evening hunt was about to begin!

We found the herd in our binoculars and watched to see what they were going to do. They got up and started walking down the canyon. The thermals were still going up, and the elk were using that to their advantage.

I waited in anticipation hoping that we had played the game right, but to our frustration the elk made their way to the other watering spot. We totally guessed wrong!

"Well, you were right that they were going to go to water before they went down to the meadow to feed," said Jack.

We watched them through our binoculars. The king was walking through the water. He splashed water with his giant antlers as he turned his head from side to side. Water droplets dripped off his tines. It was such a cool scene! I wish I had a camera to capture what I saw. Then the king worked his way out of the water, and started pushing the herd of cow elk towards the meadow. He stretched his neck out and bugled.

"Hey Jack, do you think I could bugle to him?" I asked hopefully.

He shrugged, "Why not? Let's see if you can pull him away from his cows over this direction. Where we are now, we're not really in a position to make a move on them anyway."

I pulled out my grunt tube and put my diaphragm in my mouth. I wasn't 8 anymore. I couldn't just use my voice to make the bugle sound like I did the last time I bugled with Dad. My voice was now too deep to hit the high sounds that I would need to hit in order to get the bulls attention.

I let her rip. I started deep with a growl, and then went up with a high-pitched shriek. It wasn't as good as Jack's bugle, it probably sounded more like a weak spike than a potential challenger. We watched the king through the binoculars. It looked like he at least heard my bugle, and he acknowledged it by taking a few steps in our direction.

He responded with a monster bugle. He did not like the fact that another bull might even be contemplating making a move on his cows. He turned his head back and forth slowly trying to locate the bull that had dared bugle in his domain. He trotted a few steps in our direction. My heart leaped a little thinking that he might actually leave his cows and come to us. The king was about 250 yards away from us. If this was rifle season I'd have the perfect shot, but he was way too far for my bow. The king stopped walking towards us, and went back to feeding.

Jack told me to stay put, and that he would move back and start a bugling sequence.

"Hopefully I can get that bull to walk right past you," he said.

Before he left, he whispered, "If he does come. Don't look at those monster antlers. Just focus on the spot behind his shoulder. Stay calm. Don't be a Looky Loo. Follow through with your shot. I believe in you."

With those words of advice, he started making his way back behind me. When he reached a spot about 100 yards from me, he let a beautiful bugle sound through the canyon.

The king bull raised his head, and let out an angry, powerful bugle. It was amazing to hear. He started trotting closer to me. He was now 200 yards and closing in. My heart started beating faster. I took a few deep breaths and told myself to calm down. Jack bugled again, but this time he followed his bugle with raking a tree. That did it. It was like the prideful king was on a string coming towards me. Everything was working perfectly according to plan.

Then without warning, the walls of the canyon were filled with the most terrifying bugle I've ever heard. The sound reverberated off the canyon walls. I was so confused. It wasn't the king. It for sure wasn't Jack....

Suddenly, the challenger from earlier came crashing into the meadow. He was full of adrenaline, but more importantly he was full of determination. The king stopped coming towards us, and put all of his attention on this young strong bull that would not give up. The challenger put his head down, and with all of his might charged the king bull. Their antlers clashed for the second time today. The crash of their antlers made the most amazing sound. The challenger had his head lower than the king, and had the early advantage. He lifted with his powerful neck. The king bull took three steps backwards. He tried to disengage his antlers to get a better position like he did the previous time, but this time the challenger wouldn't let him. He kept pushing with all of his might.

The king bull was in trouble. He was not ready for such a ferocious fight. However, he dug in deep and stopped the forward momentum that the challenger had created. They were locked in a stand still. Their antlers rattled as they jockeyed for position. Both of these majestic bulls were determined to not give in to the other. They fought until they both were breathing so loud that I could hear them nearly 200 yards away. Then it happened....

CHAPTER 28

THE SHOT

The challenger twisted his antlers just right, and pushed at the same time with all of his might. The king's knees buckled underneath him, and he went down to the ground. I could not believe what I was seeing. The king had fallen! The king had fallen! The challenger drove his antlers into the crumbled body of the now vulnerable king. He pulled back, stood over the downed monarch, then let out the most magnificent bugle. It was his crowning call. Devil's Canyon had a new king.

The fallen king stood up with a stagger. Through the binoculars I could see that he was hurt badly. Blood was streaming from behind his left shoulder. The new king's antlers must have penetrated his fallen enemy's body. With blood pouring out of his shoulder, he turned towards my position and started to run downhill towards the water hole.

I didn't know what to do. He was coming, and he was coming fast. I decided to draw back my bow. The injured bull would be in shooting range in seconds. I tried to find him in my sights, but there was no way I was going to try to shoot at a moving target. I almost panicked, but instead I dug down deep and composed myself.

My mind started to think clearly. The whole world slowed down for a moment. I felt the diaphragm still in my mouth from when I bugled earlier. I used it to make a sharp cow call. The bull stopped for an instant to see what had made that sound. As he stopped my sight fell to the perfect spot behind his right front shoulder. I focused my sight on an individual hair, and gently pulled the trigger on my release. I followed through the same way I did that day that I Robin Hooded my arrow in the bullseye.

My arrow flew true. It penetrated the bull's hide exactly where I had aimed. I watched as the veins on my arrow disappeared into this truly magnificent creature. He turned away from me, leaped into the air, then ran up the south side of the canyon. Within seconds I heard the crashing sound of a dead bull elk.

Jack came running from his calling position. The moment he got to me he wrapped his arms around me.

"You did it, James! I couldn't be more proud of you! You handled that moment like a true hunter. You were calm and collected. You didn't take a shot at a running elk. Your idea to make a cow call to stop him was incredible. Then you made a truly perfect shot!!!"

I stood up and put my hands behind my head and started pacing back and forth breathing deeply. My body was filled with energy, it was coursing through me. My eyes were open wide with excitement. The weight of having to shoot a bull was lifted from my shoulders.

"I can't believe that happened. I've never felt so much adrenaline in my life. I'm so happy. It feels like I am floating! Did I really just shoot the king? Am I dreaming?"

Then a new thought entered my mind, "Did you see where he went after I shot him?" I asked.

"I didn't see him fall, but I sure heard him hit the ground hard. Let's give him a little longer to make sure we don't spook him back up if he's not dead yet. Where was he when you shot him?" asked Jack.

We walked over to the spot where my bull stood when I made the shot. I was still breathing hard. The king was right at 20 yards from where I had taken the shot. There was bright red blood splattered all over the canyon floor.

"Bright red blood is a great sign. It usually means a lung shot. Do you see the little bubbles in the blood? said Jack.

We looked around, and found my arrow. I was really, really hoping that it was still in one piece. I found it sticking out of the ground in the mud. I had shot him straight through. The blood on the arrow matched the blood on the ground. It was bright red, and covered in little bubbles. I put the arrow back into my quiver.

"I'm going to say you double lunged him! It's been long enough now. Let's see if we can find your trophy before it gets too dark!" exclaimed Jack.

We followed the blood trail up to the point of the canyon wall where my bull disappeared. The ground was torn up, and the blood trail was easy to follow. I looked up and saw him. There he was in all his majestic glory.

Jack told me to approach him from behind, and make sure he was dead. I walked up above his body, and tapped his backside with my bow. He was dead. I quickly went and grabbed the base of his antlers. They were so thick that my 12-year-old hands couldn't even go around them. I started to cry.

This time it was a cry full of happiness and relief. I had fulfilled my mission to harvest a bull elk to provide meat for my struggling family. I thought of the look of desperation in my dad's eyes. I knew that this special animal would provide much needed nourishment for my family. I put my head down and whispered to this majestic fallen king.

"Thank you for giving your life for my family. You have no idea how much you mean to me. Thank you. Thank you. I will always remember you, and the way you held your head high as **The King of Devil's Canyon**."

Jack came over. This time I wasn't ashamed to let him see me cry. To my astonishment there were tears coming from his light blue eyes as well.

CHAPTER 29

MOMENT OF REFLECTION

We spent the next few moments soaking up all the emotion of accomplishing such a tremendous feat together. I looked up into the sky. The sun was setting. We decided that we should start processing my bull to make sure we preserved the meat. It would be a lot easier to do this messy task in the light of day. Jack walked me through the gutting process. It was not very much fun. It was actually pretty gross, but I learned a ton about the anatomy of an elk.

"James! You're not going to believe what I just found!" exclaimed Jack.

"What did you find?" I asked

"Look at this!" Jack said as he pointed to the spot behind his left front shoulder.

Lodged in the bull's hide was a broken off antler.

"Is that from the challenger?" I asked excitedly.

"It is! Look at how deep it went! It made it all the way to his lung. This bull was already going to die before you ever even took your shot!" Jack declared.

I pulled the piece of the challenger's antler out of the body of the bull. It was a good seven inches long. My heart was full. I was so grateful to have something to remind me of my special moments with the challenger. I put the broken tine into my pocket right next to my True Hunter coin.

After we processed the bull, we decided to quarter him so that we could get him out of this canyon. We decided that we would sleep in the canyon tonight in our hammocks, and start the rigorous process of packing out the bull early in the morning. We put the elk quarters into cotton bags that Jack had brought to keep the meat clean. We went down to the pond and cleaned off our gross hands.

I saw my reflection in the pond. I was dirty, and bloody, but what I saw was deeper than the surface. I saw a young man that had overcome failure. I was truly proud of the face that I saw.

We hung up our hammocks. By this time the sun had gone down, and we were surrounded by darkness. Our bodies were tired and worn out. It was hard to even get into the hammocks. The canyon was silent for several moments. Neither of us spoke. Suddenly, an earth-shattering bugle came from the newly appointed King of Devil's Canyon.

"Jack?" I said.

"Yes, James?"

"This was the best day of my life," I stated.

"You know what, James, it was the best day of my life too," Jack said in a very solemn voice.

Jack continued, "I've never told you this before, but about 30 years ago I had a wife and a baby son. I loved them both with everything in me. I still do in fact. They both died in a car accident when my son was not even a year old. Ever since then, I wondered what it would have been like to take my son hunting with me."

He paused for a few seconds and said, "Now I know." Another tear fell from his tender eyes.

We didn't speak another word that night, but both of our hearts were full with love and gratitude to the other. Hunting does that to you. It knits you together in a way that you'll always feel connected.

CHAPTER 30

DRAGGING ANTLERS

We woke up early the next morning, and started the extremely challenging hike back to camp. Each of us took a quarter of the elk. It was going to take two trips to get all the meat back to the camper. I wanted to take the antlers on my pack. We tried tying them on my pack, but they were taller than me. They dragged on the ground when I tried to walk, so Jack had to take them. I watched in awe as they dangled downwards from the top of his pack. As we started our accent out of the canyon, we looked back at the canyon floor through our binoculars. I found the newly crowned King of Devil's Canyon. He raised his head high, and bugled another royal bugle. I looked at his antlers, and saw where his tine was broken off.

That tine was now in my pocket. I had so much admiration for him. I would always remember him, and the experiences that we shared together deep in Devil's Canyon.

We spent all day packing my bull out of the canyon. After the first trip to the camper, we both collapsed. We laid on the ground for at least a half of an hour. The realization that we would be heading back to the bottom of the canyon shortly to get the other half of my bull was almost too much for my brain to take in. I could barely move. My body had never felt so tired. Jack looked like he would be able to sleep for a week.

We stood up and put the two quarters of my bull into coolers that Jack had brought for our trip. Then Jack looked at me and asked if I was ready to get the rest of my bull. I looked at him with tired eyes, but then a smile came across my face.

"Hey Jack, remember when the challenger gave both of us elk fever?"

Jack stood up straight and said, "Do you remember the sound when the king and the challenger's antlers clashed for the first time?"

All the way down the canyon and all the way back up we shared our newly made memories with each other. The memories gave us the will power to move on and finish what we had started.

We hitched up the camper so we could make our way back home. Jack opened his squeaky truck door and got in the truck. I realized I was so excited to see my parents!

On the drive home Jack said, "James, I am so so thankful that you missed that spike on opening morning!"

I laughed, "You know what? I am too! We would have missed out on the hunt of a lifetime if I had not failed."

"You turned a failure into a success. You could have chosen to give up, but you didn't. You and the challenger bull are made out of the same material. You know what I mean? You both failed, but did not give up, and you both ended up victorious in the end!" he stated.

CHAPTER 31

HOME

We drove down the main road of my neighborhood. The antlers were in the back of the truck, but they stood so tall that the whole neighborhood could see them. Some of the jerk neighborhood kids were playing in the street.

They ran over and said, "Hey Coach! Is that your bull? He's humongous!"

Jack leaned back in his seat so the kids could see me sitting in the passenger seat.

"Actually, James shot this trophy bull. He used a bow that he bought himself. You should have seen the masterful shot he made. He is a True Hunter if I've ever seen one."

Then Jack drove off as cool as can be, and left the kids picking their jaws up off the pavement. We pulled into my driveway. I looked at the scarred pine tree that the lightning had struck the night of the hunt lottery. I shook my head in amazement.

I got out of the truck, and grabbed the arrow that I had used to shoot the King of Devil's Canyon. I walked up to the front door that had a fancy glass window in it. I rang the doorbell. I stood there in my camo clothes and held my arrow in front of me. My parents both came to the door together. They saw me through the window holding the bloody arrow. Their faces both lit up as they realized what they were seeing. They opened the door as fast as they could.

"You shot a bull?" Dad asked excitedly.

"I did!" I exclaimed.

They both threw their arms around me, and hugged me as tight as they could.

Through the tight squeeze I said, "I told you I'd bring home the meat!"

The feeling was euphoric. They were so happy. Then my mom pushed me away.

"You stink! Did you get sprayed by a skunk?"

I shrugged my shoulders and said, "Maybe."

We all laughed together.

The End

CHAPTER 32

EPILOGUE

Things were different after my time in Devil's Canyon. The meat from the king filled up the whole freezer in our garage. We were able to have amazing, healthy meals every night. Have you ever had elk meat? It's incredible! The money my parents saved in groceries helped us all get through a hard time financially.

Word got out about the 12-year-old that shot a world class bull out of the bottom of Devil's Canyon. The news spread wide and far. My picture with "The King" even ended up in a couple hunting magazines. People from all over wanted to hear my story and see my bull.

My dad's ankle healed up perfectly. He was right that he would have a sweet looking scar! He was able to get back to work and provide for our family. He even got a raise which helped him catch up on the bills. We talk all the time about getting drawn again for Devil's Canyon. He says that it's his turn to join the ranks of the brave hunters willing to hike to the bottom of the canyon.

Jack basically became a second dad to me. I told him that he could take his new son hunting anytime he wanted! He paid to get "The King" mounted for me as a present. The King of Devil's Canyon hangs high on our wall. The memory of OUR bull will live on for generations.

Next to the magnificent mount is a smaller mount that I made. I took the challenger's 7-inch broken antler, and glued it to a short piece of oak. To me, this mount means just as much as the giant king bull that hangs next to it.

It's a reminder to me of what pure determination can accomplish. The challenger failed, but he rose to become the new King of Devil's Canyon. It also reminds me of how I once failed, but rose up and succeeded at bringing home the meat for my family.

Maybe someday I'll get a chance to hunt the "New" King of Devil's Canyon....

ABOUT THE AUTHOR

"The bull I would have jumped over if my dad hadn't ruined my moment"-Clint Ellsworth

Clint Ellsworth was born with a bow in his hand. He hiked Devil's Canyon when he was 2. He put up his first tree stand by himself before he could even talk. Actually, none of that is true, except the part where he was born. But... Clint did grow up in a family where hunting was a way of life. He now has his own hunting family that includes 5 ridiculously awesome kids. He loves hunting so much, he started writing to share his adventures with kids around the world.

Clint also makes videos for kids who love the outdoors. You can check out his hunting tips and tricks, arrow and bullet tests, funny songs, and maybe even a few explosions at
TrueHunter.com

Made in United States
Orlando, FL
02 December 2024

54866171R20085